The Russian Connection

Release 1.20

Second of the Mick Grundy Thrillers
by

Alexander Francis

The Russian Connection

Copyright ©2014 by Alexander Francis
Arcus Verba Publishing
P.O Box 210
De Forest, Wisconsin
53532
www.arcusverba.com

TM

Cover design by Alexander Francis

Graphic images from Wikipedia and modified personal photographs

ISBN: **978-1-942420-11-8** print edition
ISBN: **978-1-942420-10-1** e-book

Table of Contents

Other Mick Grundy Thrillers

The body was still in the car, and Simon leaned in with Jonny's flashlight in one hand. Its passenger was partially upright, but his pants and underwear were down around his knees. The lower part of the face was missing with the upper teeth exposed like some kind of upside down white picket fence. Blood and tissue fragments mixed with glass shards were throughout the car.

The Lieutenant pulled back and stood up. "Damn," he said.

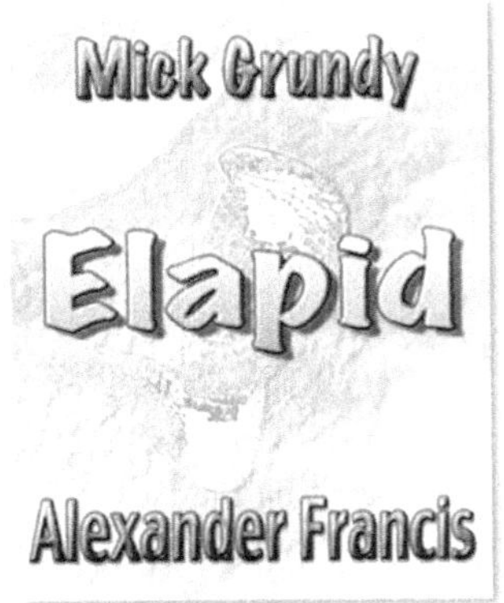

"What are we supposed to do now?" Ahmed asked not too quietly, continuing to play nervously with the safety on his rifle.
"Plainly, we are about to die. We have executed a plan doomed to fail from its inception. Mick Grundy will kill us, and we have only ourselves to blame. We came looking for him only to find his shadow, and now we have run out of options."

Read Excerpts from other novels by Alexander Francis
Visit afnovels.com

Are We A Band Yet?....Beware the Exit....The Green Scarf Revenge of Jesus....Geminknot....Anthology of Childhood Schemers and Dreamers.....Memory Gap

Chapter 1

First Contact

Point Defiance Park Zoo, Tacoma
0100 hours

It was the click of metal against metal that awakened him. His ears were ahead of his brain, and as he quickly emerged from sleep, his mind couldn't place the sound, other than to know that he heard it. He silently pulled the covers back and pivoted to an upright position and listened. Another sound occurred, different from the normal nocturnal sounds of animals moving around. Human. There was a nearby growl and cough from the big cat cage. They also heard a strange sound and sensed that there was something amiss. Mick slid his hand under his pillow, withdrew his 45, and stood up. Another sound, closer this time and coming his way.

Mick had taken up sleeping in the park zoo the last several months, after getting informal permission from the park director, who owed him a favor. He knew that, eventually, someone would see him, and he would have to move on. He liked it in the zoo, and the animals were used to him now. When weather permitted, he usually slept in an unused outside cage reserved for the Asian Tiger, currently empty until a replacement cat could be found. It was an ideal sleeping spot, with fresh air off the nearby water and an incomparable alert system provided by the animals.

Mick waited as footsteps approached. Someone was trying very hard to be stealthy. He guessed that the sound that wakened him was probably a lock being cut on one of the park's side gates. Or it could have been the sound of a round of ammo being chambered. A shadow moved toward his pen as Mick watched, gun in hand. The shadow eased up to his enclosure and peered inside, clinging to the fence wire with his fingers passing through the mesh.

Mick spoke, "Don't move. Freeze right there." The sound of his voice usually sent a spine tingling chill through most people who heard it for the first time, and this was no exception.

"Don't shoot, *por favor*. I'm seemply the messenger," the shadow said.

"What do you want," Mick asked. His voice was rough, like stone over stone, and as demanding.

"You are *Señor* Grundy, yes?" The shadow-man, as

directed, didn't dare move. There was no response from Mick, who stood silently waiting for a reply. There was a rattling sound from the fence wire as the man started shaking. "Señor, I am sent by the lady to get you to follow so that she may speak to you, that is all. I am not armed."

"What lady," the voice rattled.

"*Por favor, Señor.* She waits by the outside fence."

"Is she alone?"

"*Si, Señor.* She is alone. There is no other."

Mick studied shadow-man before answering. "Turn loose the fence and turn around. I will come around the building and tell you when I am ready. Do not try to run, or I will catch you, and you will become breakfast for the lions." There was a well-timed muffled growl from the lions nearby, which made the point more evident. The man followed instructions, stepped back, and put up his hands and waited. After a few moments, Mick Grundy silently appeared behind him.

"Lead," the voice commanded, and they walked slowly toward the outside fence under the trees. The shadow-man couldn't tell how far in front he was. He was starting to get a bad feeling about living through this job and now knew that fifty bucks was not enough. As they approached the side gate, the cut lock hanging from its hasp, he stopped and started looking both ways for the lady with the accent who had hired him. She was not in sight, and he felt a cold sweat break out on his forehead. He turned to look for this Grundy fellow, but he also wasn't in sight. For a moment, he just stood there with his hands in the air looking longingly at the closed gate and thought about how long it would take him to open it and bolt across the parking lot for the woods on the other side.

"Try it, and I'll shoot you in the back of your head," the voice behind him said softly.

The shaking returned, and the shadow-man stood there with his hands describing small arcs in the night air. The shadows from the fence played across his face as he fought his body's urge to faint. In the distance, a peacock's cry hung in the night air. There was a subtle motion from the other side of the fence, and a woman's silhouette appeared, framed by yellow light cast from tall poles standing guard in the parking lot.

"You can let him go now, and we can talk," the woman said.

Mick cautiously looked around before responding. "Who are you?" he asked.

Instead of answering him, she said, "Jose, you have done well. Go now."

Jose waited with his hands in the air, but no permission to leave was granted from behind him. Hesitantly at first, he slowly lowered his hands, and when there was no reaction, he moved toward the gate, gaining speed as he realized that he could go. He left the gate open as he fled rapidly for the tree line and disappeared into the darkness.

"Mick Grundy, I presume. You are the hardest person to find in North America. I have been looking for you for a long time," she said. There was only the sound of the park animals from the other side, and try as she might, she could not discern where Mick was standing. She waited for a response, but became aware that he was waiting for her to answer his question. "My name is Sasha, and I have been instructed to contact you and convince you to go to a meeting with my superior."

A deep, foreboding voice came floating through the fence, "Is your superior Russian like you?

She hesitated. "Yes, but I have to qualify the answer." She began to add something but was cut off.

"I don't work with Russians. We don't have a good history together. Are you alone?" the voice asked.

"Yes."

"If I find that you lied to me, you will never leave this place."

Sasha felt a chill. "There is a driver in the car. No others, I promise." She could sense, better than see, a large shape looming just inside the gate. He was within arm's reach, but she still could not make out his face.

"What do you want of me?" the shape asked. The voice was closer this time.

Before she could answer, the shape grasped her arm, pulling her inside the gate and closing it behind her. They walked silently away from the fence but kept inside the tree line, where it was the darkest.

Sasha felt her lip quivering. It was dead cold in the woods, and she admitted to herself that she was never more afraid than at this moment. Mick Grundy let go of her arm and turned her to face him. She detected a strange earthy odor about him that, normally, she would find very appealing. He was close enough that she could feel the air move when he breathed. On the other side of the park fence, the waves gently lapped at the shore. "Are you going to hurt me?" she asked. Perhaps he was still deciding, she reasoned, but the lack of response of any kind was intimidating. "I am Russian, as you have detected. At one time, I served in the GRU in Russia, and all of us there knew about Mick Grundy. You are legend, and not a good one. But there are some Russians who feel that the country is headed in the wrong direction and that we are headed back into the dark times when the KGB and the Communist Party ruled. We are trying to get it back a little at a time. There is a lot I could tell you, but I hope that you will meet with my superior, who would like some help from you. You have nothing to fear from us, because we feel that you always have done what needed doing, however rough the methods you chose." She paused to swallow and try to calm down. The dark shape in front of her hadn't moved, and except for the warm breath, she could be standing in front of a tree trunk and wouldn't know the difference.

"If you know my history, you know that I could never trust Russians. Your people killed my wife and nearly killed me, twice. I can never forgive you. Never." The voice that came at her was deep and fractured, like a broken speaker cone. When he stopped talking, the jungle sounds continued as a low murmur behind them.

"Most Russians are good people, but the few who are in control of the country right now are not. They conspire to cause war in the Middle East to stop the flow of oil to the West, simply to enrich the oil barons in Russia and their communist puppet masters. They seek to destabilize the United States and the countries of Europe and to weaken them to prevent a response to Russian aggression. Right now, they are supplying terrorist states like Iran and Syria with weapons and advisors to assist spreading Islamic Fundamentalism all over the globe. We get no help from your intelligence agencies who have to cooperate with 'Official Russia'."

"How does any of that have anything to do with me?" he asked.

She nervously cleared her throat before continuing. "We know that you have contacts in the CIA and the German BND, and we know what you are capable of from previous experience. You can do things that no one else can do. We are willing to do anything you ask and pay any price you demand. Please come and talk with us and learn more before making up your mind."

"How did you find me?"

She hesitated to answer and stammered "Well, uh."

"Trust you? Why should I trust you or work with you, if you won't even answer a simple question?"

"Okay," she said. "We know that you do PI work from time to time. After all, you advertise in the phone book. One of your recent clients was actually a set-up to find you. We started following you and finally put a tracking device on your motorcycle. When we found that you often came here at night, we bribed some of the staff who told us where you slept."

"Which client?" Mick asked.

Again, she hesitated. He silently waited, and she knew that she would either have to answer the question or face unknown consequences. "Ronald McFadden," she finally said.

"That fellow supposedly shot his wife, and I helped his defense attorney prove that he had an alibi. You people set all that up just to find me? That means that your people killed his wife. You are no different than the Russians you want to replace."

She replied, "The wife was GRU and was about to turn in her husband. He is one of us, and we couldn't afford to lose him."

"God, you Russians are devious. I don't want anything to do with you. You are all covered with the same filth. You can leave, but don't ever contact me again, and if I ever suspect you or your people are trailing me, you will find that my reputation is justified. Now get away from me."

Sasha turned to leave, but felt his large hand grasp her shoulder and she stopped. He pulled her small purse from her shoulder and felt around inside of it searching for something. He found the small flashlight he knew would be there and used it to light her face.

"I want to get a good look at you before you go," and he used the flashlight to study her face. He found a remarkable beauty before him, with long, dark hair and green eyes. Her lips were full and the short upper lip turned up slightly giving her a pouty but very appealing face. "Typical of them to send a beautiful woman on a mission like this. You ever wonder if they care that you might get killed?" he asked. She didn't answer, instead continuing to stare at the dark shape before her. "I've seen enough. Now get out of here," he said and pushed her purse into her chest.

Sasha walked away without looking back, her hips seductively swaying as she crossed the empty parking lot, gradually fading out of sight. Mick waited at the gate until he heard a car start in the distance and drive away. He went back to his cage and tried to sleep, but he knew that this was the last night at the zoo for him, and in the morning, he would have to leave. He reminded himself to look for the tracking device on his motorcycle before riding away.

Chapter 2

Chapter 2

Old Friends

Point Defiance *Park Zoo, Tacoma*
0730 hours

Mick went about cleaning up, putting his bed away for good. He had few personal belongings with him at the park, and they all fit into a small leather satchel. He bent over his motorcycle and studied it carefully before finding a small device attached behind the rear license plate. After searching the bike two more times, he finally decided that it was clean. He had acquired the bike in Germany, and he and his friends put it together, one piece at a time. The motorcycle, at its heart, was a dedicated racing machine and could easily and quickly reach over 200 miles an hour. Mick also had acquired the motorcycle skills that you can only get on a race track under expert tutelage. He tied the bundle to the rear of the bike and headed over to the food stand to get his usual breakfast.

Rita was busy starting up her grill in the small park cafe as Mick came up and sat down at the counter. She looked up and smiled, "Good morning, my fine animal friend! Have the usual?" Without waiting for a response, she turned her back on him and busily continued with her preparation.

Mick studied her back for a while in silence before deciding, "It was you, wasn't it?"

Rita turned and looked him in the face, "How did you know, Mick?" She started forming tears, her lip quivering as they trickled down her face. She was middle-aged and overweight and looked sad and tired. Cursed by poor vision, she wore thick, dirty glasses which balanced near the tip of her nose.

"Don't worry, Rita. I would never be upset at you. I just want to know what they told you to get your cooperation and what they paid to get it."

"An attractive woman came up to me a couple of days ago and said that she knew that Mick Grundy was staying here, and she needed to talk to him about saving her sister from beatings by her boyfriend. She said that she was afraid that her sister was going to get killed by this man and that the police were of no help. She cried and cried, and I felt so sorry for her. She promised that she only wanted to talk to you, and if she knew where in the park you stayed, she would wait there until you arrived. I didn't want any money from her, but she insisted on giving me forty dollars. I hope you are not angry at me, Mick."

"No, dear, I'm not. I saw the lady last night and took care of her problem. She won't be back."

Rita looked relieved and smiled limply at him, and then continued to rapidly make Mick's usual breakfast.

After eating, Mick smiled at Rita again and patted her hand. "I won't be seeing you for a while, old girl. You stay healthy, you hear?" He got up and unhurriedly strolled away before noticing a flashing blue light through the trees in the direction of the park entrance and headed that way. Just beyond the main gate, two patrol cars were staggered ahead of and behind a large dark sedan, awkwardly askance across the sidewalk. There were several uniformed policemen scattered about and one detective, obviously in command. Mick moved toward the scene and got immediate attention from all of them.

"What's up, Pat," Mick called to the man in the suit.

"Well, Mick! You are most unexpected. What in the world are you doing here at this time of morning?" Detective Denby smiled at him and stuck out his hand for a shake.

"I used to stay around the park until recently, Pat. Looks like you have a homicide here." A yellow tape line fluttered in the light wind, and legs hung from the front seat behind the open car door.

"Seems like some sort of hit. The driver got it as he was attempting to exit the car. We have his ID, but there are no records of him, other than his driver's license. There is a witness, of sorts, who saw a woman running about a block away. We don't know yet if there is a connection. The time that she was seen running is close to the time of death set by the crime lab guys over there."

Mick looked around again, then asked, "Does the victim have a Russian sounding name?"

Denby stopped and looked sharply at Mick, "Yes, it's Petrov, Victor Petrov." How did you know that. By the way, where were you when this took place?"

"Don't get weird, Pat. You know I didn't shoot the guy. I had an unannounced visit in the park last night from a woman who wanted to employ me. I refused. She gave her name as Sasha, but don't count on that being her actual name. Otherwise, I don't know anything about your dead guy. We never met."

Denby rubbed his chin, "That's more than we knew a moment ago. Both Russian names. They have to be connected. What did she want, Mick?"

"She really didn't say, Pat. We didn't get very far with our conversation. She went on briefly about issues in the Russian Intelligence Service. I threw her out of the park. By the way, she is really good looking, if that helps."

"Just what I need. Intelligence issue, huh?" Denby said. He turned to see a new arrival walking toward him.

"Simmons. Just the man I wanted. Get on the radio and tell them to give the FBI a call. This might be their stray dog here," Denby ordered. He turned back to talk to Mick but realized that he had turned around and was heading back into the park. Denby shrugged. They could find him again if they had to. He must be living in the park somewhere.

When Simmons returned, he waited with Detective Denby as the crime scene was photographed and the body removed. The victim had been shot in the head at close range with a small caliber round, and there was little blood.

"Call in the Feds, Simmons?" Denby asked.

"They patched me through to a female agent who was most interested. She isn't far from here and should be here momentarily."

"Great," Denby said. "The body is leaving now. There are no witnesses and no evidence. We could just talk on the phone and give her what we have, which is nothing." As he spoke, they both turned to see a shiny black unmarked car stop just behind one of the patrol cars. A woman in a grey suit emerged from the car, and both men stood helplessly looking at her swaying figure approach them.

She walked purposefully toward the two detectives and smiled. "Special Agent April Chauncy, FBI." She didn't offer her hand and stood waiting for an expected summary. Normally, they would demand to see a badge or ID before accepting her as who she claimed to be, but there was something about her that changed the usual dynamics. She was perfect, almost in a plastic way. She had a perfection of form, features and voice, which could only be described as a robot from the future. She looked back and forth between the two men with a little smile, as if she had seen this reaction previously. "Is there a problem, Detectives? Can you go over what you have for me?" she asked politely.

Waking up, Denby said, "Forgive me, Agent Chauncy. I was just thinking about something, and we weren't expecting you so soon."

"Special Agent Chauncy, Detective," she said with her little plastic smile.

"Of course, Special Agent. Forgive me again." Before giving a summary, he looked around as if to make sure not to leave anything out. Before he could speak, there was a sound of a powerful motorcycle starting somewhere close by. Instinctively, the three looked toward the sound, and a black motorcycle with a black-clad rider emerged, following the footpath leading into the park, and came by them, rapidly gathering speed. In an instant, the bike disappeared into the distance, leaving only the faraway shriek of the motor.

"Well, there goes one of our, excuse me, your witnesses," Denby said. "Given past experience, you won't find him again unless by luck."

Special Agent Chauncy squinted into the distance, as if she could still see something, and then turned to Denby and said, "Who was that, Detective?" The smile had disappeared.

"That was a fellow called Mick Grundy. He is a colorful local PI with an interesting history," Denby answered.

Simmons piped up, "Wow, that was him? I wondered when you were talking to him who the hard guy was. He is a legend, that's for sure."

Denby remarked, "He is one tough fellow, Simmons. I want to tell you right now to never try to arrest him if you have any brains. Even if he lets you take him in, you will find yourself over your head in obnoxious CIA types, who will stick a hot poker up your ass as soon as they hear about it."

"What did Grundy say to you, Detective," Special Agent Chauncy said, her plastic smile returning. She was so direct and in control that Denby felt off balance by her presence. He couldn't wait for her to assume control of the case, if that is, what she wanted.

Denby took a deep breath and started his summary. "The vic has a Russian name, but an American driver's license issued by the District of Columbia. Other than that, we have no information. Fingerprints don't come back. There was a woman seen by a gas station attendant at 0130 this morning, running from this direction. An attractive woman paid a visit to Mick Grundy in the zoo over there, sometime around 0100. He states that she called herself Sasha and wanted to hire him, but he refused and sent her away. That about sums up our level of knowledge. Oh, and one last thing. Grundy said the woman was talking about 'issues' in Russian Intelligence, but didn't know any more."

Simmons asked "Say, do you think that Mick Grundy shot the guy?"

Denby shrugged, "I don't think so, he would probably have told me if he did."

Special Agent Chauncy asked, "Have you determined what type of firearm was used by the shooter?"

"No, not exactly. From the entry wound I'm guessing it was a 22 with a silencer. We couldn't find the ejected shell. The bad guy probably picked it up. A professional hit," Denby said.

"That rules out Grundy," she said. "He always uses a 45."

The two men looked at her with new respect. "Say,

do you know Mick Grundy?" Denby asked.

She smiled, with her perpetually perfect face, and said, "I've not met him formally, but there was a case in Frisco two years ago that I was involved with, and so was he. I did an extensive background check at that time. I can tell you that he speaks several languages fluently and was trained by both the Special Forces and the CIA. He has personally killed a very long list of people, almost all with a 45, though some with a knife, some by blunt trauma. As far as I am concerned, there is a no more dangerous man anywhere. He is a pet of the CIA who watches out for him. We are not sure if he actually works for them or not, but we are pretty sure that they support him financially and in other ways. He is an expert on a motorcycle and can disappear like a cloud of smoke. He was nearly fatally injured in Germany, and his new wife was killed. He blames Russians and hates them intensely. I am surprised the woman got away at all last night."

Denby said, "I suspected as much. We all know that he is connected. A few unfortunates around here and in Seattle, who had an occasion to fight him, have all ended up in the hospital with severe injuries. I see him around on occasion, but I would have no idea where to find him, and frankly, I don't want to try."

"So you say that this girl was meeting him in the zoo after hours? What do you make of that?" Special Agent Chauncy asked.

"I am not even able to guess about that, Special Agent. Frankly, I was hoping that you would like to take this case over. Its seems more in your area than ours. What about it?" Denby asked, grinning at her.

She smiled back, "We don't know enough to make that judgment yet. Keep working on it, and I'll be in touch." She turned on her heel and walked away, with the two men staring at her figure as it receded.

Simmons asked, "Now what?"

Denby rubbed his chin. "We file a report and forget about it. Whether she likes it or not, this case belongs to Special Agent Chauncy."

After leaving the zoo, Mick rode around for a while thinking about last night's events. Perhaps Sasha was telling the truth, and there was infighting in the Russian Intelligence Service. Someone killed the driver, and it wouldn't have been Sasha who had to run away on foot. If that were the case, she is fleeing for her life, and she has the same Russians after her who are after him. Well, there was nothing he could do about it, even if he wanted to. He decided to let the cops do their job. He caught a glimpse of the woman in the suit talking to Denby on his way past and remembered seeing her a couple of years ago in San Francisco. FBI, as he recalled, but he couldn't remember her name.

He decided on a course of action and headed across Tacoma, past the wharf area, and turned toward the other peninsula on the opposite side of the city from the zoo. Browns Point was populated with large upscale homes, particularly on the waterfront side. He slowly advanced up Tok-A-Lou Avenue looking at the numbers. A large grey complex hovered on the edge of the cliff, set well back from the street. Two large stone pillars flanked the drive toward the five-car garage. Mick turned onto the brick pavers and switched off the bike, rolling silently to the front entrance. As he was taking off his helmet and gloves, the front door opened revealing a trim woman in a soft violet-colored dress.

Chapter 3

Jennifer and Jonnie

Tok-A-Lou Avenue

About damn time you came to see us, you vagabond!" she said and ran to him, embracing him while looking up smiling.

Mick leaned forward and kissed her on her forehead and caressed her hair with his rough hand. "How have you been, Jennifer? And, how is little Jonnie?

"Better, now that you are here," she said. She held onto his waist and continued to look up at him admiringly. "Not a word in six months, Mick. We should be angry, but mostly, we are just hurt. Seeing you in the flesh again, though, makes the wait somehow worth it." She let him go and looked past him noticing the black bag on the back of the motorcycle. Her eyes twinkled a little, and she brushed away a little tear. "Does the black bag mean you are coming or going, Mick?"

"Oh, I thought if you had room in this little cottage, I would stay around for a few days and get to know you and Jonnie again."

"Oh my God, Mick, how I've prayed that someday

this would happen. We have a lot of catching up to do," she said and reached for his hand. "Well, don't just stand there. Get your little bag, and come on in." She tried to pull him toward the front door, and he let his arm stretch out and smiled at her happiness.

"One thing, Jennifer, before I go inside. I want to be your friend and your son's friend the rest of my life, if you will let me, but let's not go past that, please, for the same reasons as before."

"Please don't ask me not to love you, Mick. If you don't want to love me, that's fine, but Jonnie and I love you, and we can't help it. You saved our lives and were kind and gentle with us when we needed it, and we can never get over it. We both talk about you all the time, and you aren't going to spoil whatever short time we get to be with you by bringing up all the dangers you think follow you around. I don't care about the danger and neither does Jonnie. We just want to spend time with you, and we will relish each and every moment. Now, come inside!" Jennifer demanded and pulled harder on his arm.

Once inside, he recalled the posh entrance, the stained glass in the door, the surrounds as well as overhead. A staircase wound gently up, sheathed in figured walnut, set off by an inlayed marble floor. He marveled at the opulence, and when he looked straight ahead, past the dining room, he could see the expansive view of the bay. He chuckled to himself about the change in surroundings from last night.

"I see you laughing, you dog," Jennifer said. "Is it me or my little home you find amusing?" She typically had these put-on tifs with him, and as usual, he found her adorable for it.

"No, dear," Mick laughed out loud. "If you could see where I've been staying, you'd laugh too."

"I was going to tell you, Mick, that you have grown in odor since we last met. I can't place the smell, but it reminds me of Cracker Jacks for some reason." She wrinkled her little nose and held her hand to pinch her nostrils to emphasize the point. "Now listen, I know you by now, and I know that you won't sleep upstairs like a normal human being, so allow me show you the spare quarters over the boat shed. I know you will like it there, and maybe you will stay longer. She reached for his hand and put his arm over her shoulder, and they made their way through the house, across the patio and pool area, toward the boat house.

Mick remembered the night two years ago when they met. Her husband and young son had been kidnapped and held for ransom. The police suspected the Russian Mafia, and someone on the Police Task Force had found Mick and asked him to come into the case. When he first saw Jennifer, she had looked so small and helpless amid all the officers from the Swat Team milling about in the room. She looked at the newcomer with pleading eyes, desperation on her face. Denby was still a sergeant at the time and was the first to pull Mick aside to fill him in on the case.

"This case is typical of the Russian Mafia They grab a rich guy or his kid and ask for a big payoff. No matter what we do, they will kill the victim and may have already done so. They are very clever and completely ruthless, so if you get involved with this case, you have to proceed with a lot of caution." Mick nodded understanding and kept watching the woman during the conversation.

Mick turned to Denby and asked, "Is there going to be a payoff?"

"Yeah, Mick. They just called. They want Jennifer to carry it to the drop point. She has twenty minutes to get there. We are deciding if it's worth the risk to let her go. The drop point is over in the wharf area. She was told to leave it by a marked post in the 2000 block of Lincoln and drive away."

Mick didn't think it over very long. He walked over to Jennifer and put his hand on her shoulder. "My name is Mick Grundy, and I'm going to be with you when you deliver the money. I won't let any harm come to you. I promise." He turned to the lead detective and said, "Put an officer in the back seat on the floor of the car, just in case, and I'll follow on my motorcycle and stay with the money. After you leave the bag, just speed away, Jennifer, and I'll take it from there." His presence carried instant authority with those in the room. The voice that came out of him was like something created for the monster in a cheap Hollywood movie from the fifties.

The lead detective was Inspector Frank Jussup, and he looked shocked at the effrontery of this new guy giving orders. He blurted, "Who the hell...," but was pulled aside by one of the Swat Team who whispered in his ear. Jussup looked sheepish and shrugged. "Okay, team, you have your orders. Let's do it," and he pointed to Mick to let the others know whom to follow. He approached Mick respectfully and said, "I was just told about you, Mr. Grundy. It's a privilege to have you with us on this. I have to ask, however, if you have a plan."

Mick said, "It's simple, Inspector. I'm going to try to get the hostages back alive and kill as many of the bad guys as I can." Mick turned his back and walked away, leaving the inspector wondering if he meant it.

Shortly, they all left. The Swat Team and the other policemen set out to try to block any escape from the area. Jennifer, with an officer in the back seat, pulled out with Mick close behind on his motorcycle. As they got close to the drop site, Mick dropped back and switched off his lights. As directed, Jennifer found the post which had been covered by reflective tape in an open area at the side of the road. After flinging the satchel from the window, she pulled away quickly, and Mick discretely pulled off the road and hid in the shadow of a fence. He was wearing his black leathers and astride his flat black motorcycle was nearly invisible. Mick knew that the kidnappers couldn't wait long to give the police the additional time to organize and to set traps. From behind him, he could hear the sound of a powerful motorcycle coming his way. As he had figured, a motorcycle was the most likely choice they would make because of its speed and versatility, and a motorcycle makes a difficult target to pursue at night. That is, unless you also have one and know how to ride.

The bike came by him and braked hard at the

post. The rider leaned over and picked up the bag and rapidly accelerated. Mick turned on his lights, opened the throttle, and quickly closed the distance. It seemed to take the rider a moment to realize what was behind him, but when he did, he tossed the bag away and picked up speed. Mick's motorcycle, created for the race track, developed well over 200 horsepower and quickly overtook the other rider. As he pulled alongside, he pulled his pistol and shot once at the rear tire. The other bike instantly went down, and both the bike and its rider tumbled along the pavement in a shower of sparks before sliding into the ditch. Mick parked his bike and slowly walked toward the rider who was lying on his back, alive but dazed. He reached down, cutting the neck strap, and roughly pulling the helmet off. The man groaned and flailed slightly with his hand, evidence that he was quickly returning to consciousness. At a glance, Mick could tell that the man had a badly fractured leg, which was folded under his body at an odd angle.

Mick slapped the man in the face. "Buddy, know where you are?"

"You ain't getting nothing from me. Back off. My friends will be here soon and pay you back," the man said in heavily accented English. He was breathing heavily and occasionally groaning. Mick stood up and then stepped on the man's broken leg just above the knee, putting his full weight on it. There was a shriek, and he pounded the ground around him with his arms. Mick leaned back down and peered into the man's face.

"Unless you tell me what I want to know, I'm going to take my knife and carve you slowly into little pieces, and here's a sample," Mick said, plunging the knife deeply into the man's shoulder, then twisting it. The man screamed and pleaded for mercy.

After the interrogation was over, Mick returned to his bike and headed out with purpose. He had discovered the location of the kidnapping victims and knew that the gang was comprised of five men. They were going to kill the prisoners as soon as they got the money, probably tonight. The man on the bike was also supposed to shoot Jennifer as she left the area, and Mick's sudden appearance prevented him from carrying it out. He sped as quickly as possible toward the nearby location. The group was hiding in a cargo container near the wharf with a plan to disperse the money, kill the prisoners, and blend in with ordinary dock workers, leaving the motorcycle locked in the container.

Following Milwaukee Street, he turned into the shipping area, idling slowly down the second row, looking for container "33." He spotted it easily and parked his bike nearby. Methodically and unhurriedly, he drew his 45 from his back and took an extra magazine from his coat pocket. He pounded on the steel door and spoke in a low voice, "Откройте дверь. Я имею деньги." A small window opened, and an eye looked him over. Mick remained motionless waiting on the door to open. There was a deep clank and squeak, as the door started slowly opening. Mick pulled hard on the door, which then swung widely open. The interior was dimly lit, but Mick could make out a body on the floor and a small boy huddled in a corner. Before the man who opened the door could say a word, Mick shot him in the face and leapt into the small room, shooting the three others quickly one after another, all in the head. He went back outside and waited, gun in hand, for anyone else to show. Apparently, he had them all. Mick examined the kidnapped man's body and felt for a pulse, observing that he had been shot several times in the back. He scooped the boy up and carried him away from the scene, out into the open, where they stood, the boy clinging to him, his face buried in Mick's neck. Flashing blue lights from several directions started converging on their location, and while they waited, he stroked the boy's head and held him tightly to his chest.

"You are safe now. What's your name?" Mick asked.

The boy couldn't answer and started to shake and weep. He clung to Mick's neck fiercely, and together, they waited in the darkness of night for the police to find them. The sound of gunfire in the wharf area must have been called in, because soon they were lit up by spotlights and surrounded by uniformed police. Mick refused to let the boy go, and they rode back to his home clinging together in the back seat of a squad car.

"I'm sorry, Jennifer," Mick said, after the reunion with the boy's mother. "They shot your husband before I got there." Mick didn't seem to want to leave them and hesitantly said, "If there is anything I can do for you, please ask."

Jonnie held out his arms from his mother's lap for one last hug for Mick and then curled back up against her. Through her tears, and choking with emotion, Jennifer pleaded, "Mr. Grundy, could you stop by here tomorrow, if you have time?"

He did stop back and continued to visit them until they were able to cope with the trauma inflicted on them simply for money. After a few days, a couple of plain clothes officers paid a visit to Jennifer's home while Mick was still there.

After one of them introduced himself, he asked, "You Grundy?"

"Yes."

"We have been looking for you, but you are really hard to locate. Could I ask you a couple of questions just to clear some things up?"

They stepped outside by the patrol car. "One thing, Mr. Grundy, we don't understand. The body we found beside the motorcycle was pretty cut up. We didn't see how he could tell you where to go with injuries like that. I mean, it looks like he bled to death from cuts, not from the accident. Can you help us with that?" the officer asked.

Mick looked them both over slowly. They could feel the tension building, and the little hairs on the back of their necks started to stand at attention. Being this close to Mick made them realize just how dangerous he was. The lead officer was beginning to wish that they had not found this Grundy fellow after all.

Mick finally answered, "The fellow lived long enough to tell me what I needed to know. Riding a motorcycle at night is very dangerous. He should have been wiser, don't you agree?" They both nodded approval of his statement. "Another thing you should know, I'm not coming in for questioning."

Jennifer led the way up the stairs, and Mick was pleasantly surprised when she opened the door. The apartment was nice, very nice, and the view of the bay was magnificent. There was a small but well appointed kitchen, and it sported a large thin television positioned in front of the leather couch.

"Say you like it, Mick!" she beamed.

"Gee, Jennifer, I won't know what to do with this fancy place. I never had it so good."

"Well, you can start with staying most of the time in the other house with us. This place is for sleeping only. Now, come with me, because it's about time that we had a long talk over coffee." Again, she started pulling him along.

They sat across from each other at the table, just off of the kitchen. Jennifer brewed a pot of coffee and put out some fresh scones. The view from the adjacent window was of the pool area, the bay glistening on the other side of the stone retaining wall.

"Mick, dear, do you have any family or any sweetheart to take care of you?" Jennifer asked sweetly. In a moment like this, a woman, especially an attractive one, will extract more information from a man than any cop trained in interrogation. Mick just couldn't keep his guard up to resist her.

"I have no family in America, and there is no sweetheart," he answered.

She sipped her coffee and held him a soft but penetrating gaze. "Does that mean that you have family abroad and no sweetheart anywhere?"

"It means that since Anna was killed, I have not had a woman in my life. I couldn't bear to have another person that I love taken from me. When I came back over here from Germany, I thought I could get away from being pursued constantly, but there seems to be a lot of revenge seekers out there who won't let go."

"When she was killed, Mick...is that when you got the scars on your head and neck and what damaged your voice?"

"Yes, I almost died. For a long time, I wished that I had."

Jennifer sipped her coffee and waited for the rest. "You left out the part about family abroad," she reminded him. "Do you ever visit them, Mick?"

"Only once since I got back. It was a quick and, because I wanted to stay there with them so much, a painful trip. I was convinced by some who should know that I was bringing danger with me and putting them at risk."

"Dear Mick, will you ever find peace?" she wondered.

Mick put down his coffee and looked her in the eye. "My life, while I am awake, is a whirlpool of risk, fear, mistrust and loneliness. Each night I dream of Anna at the time of her death, and I am forever helpless to stop her from dying or to stop dreaming about it. The only possible release for me will be my own death someday."

Jennifer began to cry, and she came around the table and sat on his lap, enveloping him as she wept. "You poor man. I'll give you anything I have if it will bring you some happiness. Anything. I would love to keep you around and repay you for saving our lives at the risk of yours." At that moment, the front door opened briefly, and they could hear quick footsteps coming toward the kitchen.

"Hi, Mom," Jonnie said as he threw his school books into a corner. He did a double take when he saw Mick and his mother together. "Mick! Mick!" he blurted as he hurtled himself across the floor and jumped into Mick's extended arm. Mick pulled him forward and had both Jonnie and his mother wrapped securely and held tightly. Jonnie wiggled free and twisted around to give Mick a big wet kiss, when he noticed his mother's tears. "It's all right to cry, Mom. I feel that happy to see him, too."

"You haven't stopped growing like I told you to do. You don't listen very well, do you?" Mick asked.

"I don't listen to stupid stuff like that. Anyway, I want to be just as big as you are so I eat a lot!" He gave another wet kiss before jumping down and pulling at Mick's arm, "Come up to my room, Mick. I have something I want to show you."

"Didn't you just have a birthday, Jonnie? As I remember, that would make you eight years old!" Mick asked.

"Yes, I'm eight, and you missed my birthday." He stuck out his lower lip and scowled. "Now come upstairs," he ordered.

Chapter 4

A Call from Zeskie

Federal Bureau of Investigation
1110 3rd Avenue Seattle
0915 hours

Well, Mr. Zeskie, thank you for returning my calls...at last," Special Agent Chauncy said with thinly veiled sarcasm.

"I have a life, Special Agent Chauncy," Zeskie said. "What is the nature of your problem?"

"I am given to understand that you are the CIA handler for Mick Grundy. There are some things we need to discuss with him, but it seems no one but you can ever find him. Is this so?" she asked.

"You have been misinformed, my dear Special Agent Chauncy. Say, could I just call you by your first name? This is otherwise very clumsy, isn't it?" Zeskie observed.

Special Agent Chauncy replied, "I never use my first name when I'm working, Mr. Zeskie."

There was a moment of strained silence, then Zeskie responded, "Listen, April, my name is Ron. Now that we are proper friends, you can tell me what you want, other than where to find Mick. By the way, no one tells him what to do, especially me."

"Well, Ron, I am working on a case regarding the shooting of a Russian agent. There may be a female agent involved, and we have a rumor of a rift in Russian Intelligence. Is that interesting to you?"

"When the Russians are involved, don't believe everything you hear, April. How is talking to Grundy going to help you?"

"He told a local police officer that he talked to a young woman called Sasha. She may be the one who fled the scene of the shooting. We...I want to talk with Mick Grundy about her."

"The truth is that we have heard some things also. We are working on it, but I don't know anything about a woman called Sasha. I'll try to get a message to him for you, but don't hold your breath. If I can get through to him, I suggest that we have a meeting somewhere very secure. McChord Air Force Base is nearby, and if I can arrange it, we can meet there."

"There is also my office here at the FBI Headquarters," she suggested.

"Not a chance, April. Not a chance," Zeskie said with a laugh.

After she hung up, she looked around the room with new curiosity about hidden transmitters. She resolved to get a sweep started as soon as she could. As far as new leads on her case, she would have to wait for Zeskie to act.

Tok-A-Lou Avenue
1400 hours

Mick could hear his phone ringing in the distance. It was coming from his leather jacket, currently draped over the couch in the living room. Only a very few people had that number, and he wasn't expecting any calls. Glancing at his watch, he speculated that at this time of day, it would mean trouble. He got up and patted Jonnie on the head on the way past. Mick had been helping with homework, while Jennifer prepared the meal. Jonnie started to follow him, but Mick held up his open hand, and he sat back down.

Mick retrieved the black phone, hit the button, and put it up to his ear without speaking. "Mick, this is Ron Zeskie. Can you talk?"

"I'm listening," Mick answered.

"First of all, how the hell are you, Mick? We haven't talked for a month. Is everything going well for you?"

"About the same. Listen, Zeskie, I know you didn't call to see how I am. This is about the Russian girl, isn't it? I'm guessing that the sharp looking FBI agent called you, didn't she?"

Zeskie laughed, "I had no idea that she was good-looking. She certainly is formal and indignant, however. By the way, your brother, Peter Koffman, sends his regards. I haven't run across Kurt for some time but I recently heard that he was back at the university working on his degree. Triska is still Triska. And yes, I am calling about the Russian girl."

"You wasted your time, Zeskie, I don't know anything, and what I do know is likely a lie. Plus, if I can help it, I don't want anything to do with Russians ever again."

"That being said, Mick, could I talk you into going to a meeting at the local Air Force Base? I will have the FBI chick there and someone from Army Intelligence. There are some things going on, and you may well be the perfect man to give an opinion. Please?"

"I suppose I should do something for all the money you send, because I surely don't make ends meet being a PI. Get it into your head, however, I have most definitely not agreed to go on a mission for you, and especially to anywhere near Russia. You clear on that, Zeskie?"

"Clear as the sky, Mick, and the sun is just coming up."

"Where are you Zeskie?"

"I'm in Berlin at the moment. Need a nice pretty German blonde to snuggle up to? Say the word, and I'll go buy one and bring her with me." Zeskie laughed nastily at his own joke.

"When's the meeting?" Mick asked.

"I've got to get people lined up first. I'll let you know when I know. Okay?"

"Sure, see you then." Mick hung up and headed back to the homework assignment.

Chapter 5

The Meeting

McChord Air Force Base
1100 hours

Mick stopped his motorcycle at the guard post barricade and waited for the armed MPs to inspect him and the bike. He observed two more in the guard house, rifles at the ready.

"Your ID, sir," the larger one said, reaching for the items Mick offered. He scanned the three electronically and then held one up to see Mick's facial comparison. Turning one of them over, he softened his hard look. "Army Special Forces Lieutenant Mick Grundy, Inactive Duty. Is this correct, sir?"

"Yes, Sergeant," Mick replied.

"Where are you going today, sir?"

"You tell me, Sergeant. They didn't say where."

The Sergeant disappeared into the gate house and made a call. In a moment, he came back out. "Building 454, Room 12. Straight ahead and turn left at the first turn. You can't miss it. There is additional security in position there, sir." He saluted, and Mick returned the salute crisply.

He was searched at the next stop, and they requested permission to hold his 45 caliber pistol for him during the meeting. Mick agreed and was shown into the conference room. Zeskie and the FBI agent were huddled together in conversation. A two-star Army officer sat alone, busily looking through his open briefcase. There were two second lieutenants standing behind him, ready to assist, both in full dress uniform. He snapped to attention and held his salute until the Major General returned it.

"At ease, son. We are informal here this morning. I was just going through your file. Very impressive," the General said. He got up and came around the table toward Mick. "I am Major General Chuck Adams, but I want you to call me Chuck. I am honored to meet you, son, and here is my hand on it." He spoke with a Southern drawl and had kind eyes, but his chest was filled with campaign medals and ribbons. After Mick shook his hand, he realized that the General was in top physical condition. General Adams patted him on his arm and led him to his seat beside Zeskie, who winked at him and nodded. He leaned forward to catch the eye of the female FBI agent who mouthed a "hello" and smiled in an insincere way.

The two intelligence agency representatives, Zeskie and Chauncy, were not under the command of General Adams, but he apparently didn't care. He was in charge by his very nature and opened the conference by snapping the lid of his briefcase closed.

"Gentlemen and Lady, we are here to discuss some

recent developments which may concern the United States of America and its potential adversary, Russia." Zeskie caught Mick's attention and rolled his eyes up briefly. The General continued, "As we all know, Russia is up to its old tricks again, but this time there are some in Russia who feel that the country is making some mistakes. The Empire has shrunk, and in addition, they still offer no products to the world except raw materials and weapons. They have clients buying weapons in the radical Muslim world, and Europeans buying their energy products. They seem to have instituted a strategy to create and exploit dependence by the Europeans and foster instability and war among the Arab and Muslim states. If the dissident Russians look at the overall picture, they can't miss seeing the collection of former Soviet states clustered around their southern border which are predominately Muslim and, therefore, eventual hostiles. It is a lose-lose situation for them in the long run. Short term, however, this policy is working and is causing us a lot of problems." He looked at the seated guests to see if they were paying attention, then continued. "There are some indications of strife in the Russian GRU, and we are aware of some who have been eliminated by their comrades, but for what reason, we are not certain. Ron, would you care to add anything to this summary," he asked.

Zeskie rose to standing and said, "Thanks, General Adams, for your perceptive and accurate summary of problems the Russian people are facing. I would offer one insight based on experience. You cannot take anything you see and hear about them at face value. Collectively, they are masters of deception and have no limits about what they will do to cloak their real intentions. Regardless of the certain fact that some Russians don't like the present administration or their path, it really means very little, because they will not be able to change anything. Another glaring problem is the fact that most Russians are nationalistic and love Mother Russia. They will usually not agree to spy on their homeland, unless we force them to do so. The only opening for us to exploit would be to recruit some of the dissidents for information gathering. At least, we may be able to understand the future of our relationship. A significant issue, however, is that it is difficult to detect a double agent. This current event could be another GRU plot after all. A scheme to plant an agent who we are led to believe is working for us." He smiled at the others before sitting down.

General Adams turned to Mick and said, "Son, would you describe the meeting you had recently with the female who claimed that she was a dissident?"

Mick glanced at Chauncy, only to see her little smirk. He had no idea what she was thinking, but she appeared to have abundant hostility toward him. Leaning back in his chair, so he didn't have to look at her, he said, "General, the woman in question tracked me by an elaborate ruse which pretty well confirms what Zeskie just implied. They will use any tactic to accomplish their goal. From what this Sasha admitted to me, it's obvious that her people shot, or had shot, a married woman to bring me onto the legal defense team so that they could plant a bug on my motorcycle. While she did say that she was part of a group who are resisting the present direction of Russia, she didn't exactly explain what she wanted me to do, and anyway, I refused to work with her. It appears as though her driver was executed, and she ran away from the area, but again, reality may be different than appearances. Should she actually be on the level and on the run, she may be a useful source of information for us. My opinion, should you want to know, is that we forget about her. She is most likely bait, not a dissident. The reason I say this is because she is very attractive, and the Russians know that you catch more flies with honey than tar. The other thing I want to say is to Agent Chauncy only. I don't know why you think so highly of yourself, but if you want to work in this adult world with us, you have to tone down your ego."

Chauncy shot to her feet, and they all could see her face reddening. "I have an answer to that, General and Agent Zeskie. This man you all bow and scrape to is simply a brutal killer. He is about as useless as a tank unless you want to destroy or blow something up. I resent working with him at all, and I really don't care to hear his opinions. He is neither in the CIA nor in the military. He is just a PI who sleeps in an animal cage, has no office and nearly no belongings and here he sits like an equal." Her face continued to get redder, and she lost all her previous plastic composure. She was very angry, and her nostrils flared as she inhaled.

Mick stood and applauded, laughing as he did so. "Well, well, April, you are not synthetic after all. We were under the widely held assumption that you were a robot, but you just dropped the shell around you so we could see the real woman. Congratulations. The next thing you should try is a good orgasm."

April Chauncy was about to come to her feet again over the last remark when the General put up his hand and said, "Enough. We are here for national security issues and not to fight among ourselves. By the way, Agent Chauncy, Mick Grundy is a true national hero, whether you think so or not. It's true that he has seen his share of this brutal world, but few among us could have done what he has done or suffered so much. Unlike you, I am honored to share the room with Mick Grundy, and I deeply appreciate his advice." He turned to Mick and waggled his finger at him. "And you behave."

Zeskie spoke up again. "It seems like we should find this woman and discover what she is made of. I hate to say it, Mick, but you are the most qualified of anyone I can think of to take this on. You already know what she looks like, and if she is really on the run, you can put yourself in her shoes and perhaps track her down." He paused and looked at the others. "Of course, you have the cooperation of our combined agencies to help you do it. What do you think? Will you have a go at this?"

Mick glared at Zeskie for a long time, then answered, "Yes."

Zeskie smiled, then turned and winked discretely

at General Adams. He looked back at April before speaking. "My dear Special Agent Chauncy, I spoke to the office of the Director of the FBI yesterday. You have been assigned to work exclusively with Mick Grundy for the duration of this case. I am instructed to inform you that Mick Grundy is in charge and that you are to trust his judgment and to give him any assistance that he might require. You are, of course, welcome to check with your local supervisor to confirm this assignment which starts immediately."

Special Agent April Chauncy was so stunned by his remarks she appeared unable to close her mouth. Her wild eyes flitted back and forth trying to take it in.

Mick started laughing, "Gentlemen, please. First of all, I prefer to work alone, and being forced to work with this stuffy, haughty woman is too much. I can't see that she could be of any use and, in fact, may prevent my success by insisting on following the law to the letter. I work best in the shadows and often by inducing fear and intimidation in people. Who would be afraid of this little robotic woman?"

Agent Chauncy started shaking with anger and exploded to her feet, knocking her chair behind her with a clatter. Pushing past Zeskie, she braced and swung her right fist at Mick's face with all the force she could muster. "Slap." Her fist impacted Mick's open hand just in front of his nose.

The General stood with a raised voice, "Stop this behavior right now, you two. We can see that you don't like each other, but you have a duty to your country which is larger than your feelings." He leaned over the table with his medals and ribbons slightly swaying. "You will work together and respect each other, there is no other choice. By the way, Mick Grundy, Special Agent Chauncy has a brilliant record and an inquisitive mind. She may be smaller than you but never underestimate her. She is one tough cookie. Her perfect looks are disarming, and most people never see the blow coming until it's too late. She is more like you than you know and can blend in and be invisible when she has to. When you need her, she will be there for you." He stood back up and watched their faces intently.

Slowly, Mick rose to his feet and turned to face April Chauncy. She was still trembling with anger and refused to look at his face. "My hand is still stinging from your punch. It would have likely knocked me cold. I want to extend my sincere apologies for insulting you, and I humbly beg your forgiveness. General Adams is right, you are so beautiful that you look artificial, and I guess I couldn't take you seriously, especially since you radiated your dislike of me so clearly. You are correct, I live like an animal, smell like an animal and hide like one. I am forced to live as hunted prey from my many enemies. However, I am not an animal but a man, and I promise to give you the respect due you and treat you like a friend and partner, if you will let me."

Agent Chauncy studied Mick's face to be sure he wasn't kidding, while wiping her nose with a small tissue, then stuck out her hand for a shake. Zeskie and the General gave a soft applause and then the

General rapped on the table with enthusiasm.

Chapter 6

Partnership

Pike Street Cafe, Seattle
0700 hours

They sat in a booth across from each other for the first time and studied the small menus. April was dressed casually in jeans and sneakers, topped by a red hooded sweatshirt. A small gold charm bracelet rattled as she drank her coffee. Her long brown hair was pulled back in a pony tail, but even without makeup, she was remarkably perfect. Mick couldn't resist an occasional glance at her blue eyes when he felt that she was looking at him. He was attired in casual black slacks, a soft grey sweater with a clean-shaven face under a fresh haircut. One of Jennifer's cars, a Mercedes, was parked it front of the cafe. They ordered food and sat in silence, eating, but otherwise, the perfect couple.

What did your people find out that will help us?" Mick asked.

"Not much. The ID on the body was faked but very good. His DNA profile is Russian/Slavic. There are no fingerprints of him on record and no photos. We don't have a clue who he is or where he came from.

For Sasha, we have had a little better luck. We were able to find a cab company who picked up a woman around 0200 only two miles from the park and dropped her at a hotel in Seattle. From there, we used the security camera tapes to find the room she entered. She was gone by the time we got there, but we endeavored to collect fingerprints and DNA from the room. She is also not in our files, but Interpol did find her. She entered Germany as a Trade Delegate Assistant assigned to the Russian Embassy, seven months ago. I am told that means she is an intelligence officer. Her name of record is Sasha Romanisky. That part of what she told you was true, or at least consistent with her cover ID." April dug into the large purse she carried producing some photos and slid them across to Mick.

"That's her," Mick said. He continued to study the photos in detail. It appeared that they were taken in Germany, given the backgrounds, and by a hidden camera. They were not typical surveillance video images but nearly professional photos which caught her in various angles, both full body and close-ups of her face. Impressive. "It seems that she was on someone's list over there," Mick surmised.

"Not necessarily. The Germans are very thorough. The fact that she came into the Russian Embassy would be enough for them to be suspicious," April explained. "By the way, you clean up well." She didn't look at him when she spoke and busied herself pouring more coffee.

"Thank you, April. I would tell you that you look incredible this morning, but really you don't look any better than usual." She flicked her eyes at him and then back to what she was doing. There was a brief, faint, almost imperceptible smile that passed over her face and then was gone. Mick continued, "I think that the files from the public transportation systems should be studied to see if she left the area."

"That's being done right now," she said without looking up. "So far there are no sightings of her. We checked the morgue, the area hospitals, and the police in two states. They all have her photo by now and are looking for her."

"Well, if she left the area, she must have done it by car. But if she's still around here, she's probably hiding somewhere," Mick observed, while his chin was supported by his hand. He looked out the window in thought.

"We have the police checking all the motels and hotels for a two-hundred mile radius. We are fortunate that she is strikingly attractive and, as you said, speaks with an accent. It will help find her."

"The way I see it, April, if her training and equipment is like ours, she has several IDs that she can use and several methods of payment, including cash. Assuming that the Russians are hunting also, they would know to be alert for her to use credit cards or present an alias from her stash. If I were her, I wouldn't use anything they gave me, because they would track me down with it. I would try to avoid any place needing ID, like the rental car agencies or the large hotels. You can hide in public if you know how to blend in with the street people who are everywhere and who are never bothered. If you have enough cash, you can pay someone to take you nearly anywhere. A girl with looks like hers could take up with a man who would provide good cover unknowingly. We also need to look for whoever is looking for her. If they find her first, she is dead."

"Mick, the truth is that we don't have enough manpower to cover all the possible Russian agents out there, even if we knew who they are. I can see your point about her use of an alias known to the Russians. Given her striking appearance though, I find it improbable that she could blend in with street people anymore than I could. Your other point is the most likely. She could find a man in a bar in five minutes and encourage him to take her home with him. If she stole his car and money, she could get a good head start on us. If she killed him, it would take even longer for us to connect her, because a dead man doesn't report a stolen car."

"Let's work backwards a bit," Mick said. "Did she have any luggage with her when she left the room?"

"No," April said. "She had changed clothes and carried an oversized purse. She was wearing a dark dress with a lot of cleavage. Her luggage was still in the room. The time of exit was around 0300."

"The cabbies should be asked about picking her up at that time," Mick suggested.

"Already done. Nope, no one picked her up," April said.

"If she is on foot with no luggage, dressed for a party, she is heading to a bar within walking distance. Here is our theory in action about her being picked up. We have to act quickly because she already has a four-day head start. Let's go visit all the bars and nightclubs within walking distance and see if anyone remembers her," Mick suggested.

April quietly dug around in her bag and came out with a tablet computer and flicked it on. After a few minutes, she scribbled a list of ten possibilities. She drew a line across the middle and tore off half for Mick. "There is our list. We will work faster if we split up," she observed.

Mick studied the names on his list and said, "Room...The Med."

"What's so special about the Med Room?" April asked.

"Upscale," Mick offered. "That means a higher probability of picking up some guy with dough. Think about it, an attractive woman, provocatively dressed, shows up alone near closing time. What does she look like to the patrons and management?"

"Expensive hooker," April said flatly.

"Right. Someone will remember her. Let's go,' Mick threw down some cash on the table.

"By the way, Mick. I have an expense account so I can pay for my own breakfast."

"The CIA just bought your breakfast, and I don't use an expense account."

Room...The Med, Seattle
0930 hours

Mick found the entrance to The Med on Pine Street, just three blocks from the Convention Center. The place was closed, but he could see someone inside, probably cleaning. He banged on the door and eventually it was unlocked.

"We're closed, buddy. Don't you see the sign?" the man in the dirty white t-shirt said. He had a stubble of beard and a gut which hung over his belt. He stood blocking the door.

"Are you the only one here?" Mick asked.

"Didn't you just hear...." was interrupted by Mick's push on his chest as he came by into the room.

"Don't give me any crap. I don't have time. Is someone here in charge?" Mick said with a threatening voice.

"Down there," the man submissively said and pointed at the end of the dark hall.

Mick headed toward what was probably the office and opened the door without knocking. The couple behind the desk were in an embrace and looked up startled.

"How...Who the hell are you?" the man said as the woman got up off of his lap and started fussing with her hair.

"My name is Grundy. I am working with the FBI on a murder, and I need some information fast," Mick said. The man smoothed his long dark hair back and cleared his throat.

"All right. What do you want to know?" he said gruffly.

"Wednesday morning at about 3:00 AM...." Mick started to say.

"We close at 2:00," the man interrupted.

"Look, my friend, you can help with this, or I can get rough," Mick said. Something about his voice and body language when he spoke made his threat very believable.

"What can I tell you, man?" he said with his hands in a uplifted position.

"You can start by telling me who was working bouncer at the door and who was bartending at that time," Mick said. "I know that you stop serving drinks at 2:00, but I also know that it takes time to empty a place like this."

The manager thumbed through some papers. "We had Bob Tornston at the bar. He will be here at four this afternoon. The door man was Tom Spelling, and he is off until Saturday. You can usually find him at Gold's downtown at this time of day, working on his biceps." He looked up to see if that was enough.

Mick nodded and left the way he came in. He drove over to Gold's which was only five blocks away and entered to the familiar smells and sounds of weights being dropped, accompanied by grunts. The girl at the desk gave him a big smile. "How can I help you, sir?"

"You have a Tom Spelling working out this morning?"

She rose just enough to point out a heavily-built man in the far corner who was squatting with an enormous barbell full of weights.

Mick approached him and patiently waited for his set to be completed. As Tom was toweling off, he looked lethargically at Mick and said, "You waiting to talk to me?" He had the typical deep voice and red skin of habitual steroid use. A shiny bald head was offset by an abundant and unkempt goatee.

"My name is Mick Grundy. I am working on a

murder case and looking for a woman who might be involved. On Wednesday morning about three, she may have come to your place. She was dressed in a showy dress and very attractive.

Tom thought this over and pointed a thick finger at Mick. "What's in it for me if I remember anything?" He rose to his feet and seemed to be as wide as he was tall.

"I can spare a few bucks. Do you know anything of value?" Mick said and slowly moved toward the man.

"We'll see, first the money," Tom said.

Mick peeled off a twenty and dropped it on the floor. Tom looked down at it and remembered, "I saw a woman who wanted to get in about that time, and I refused to let her enter. She stood around for a little while outside."

"Anything else?" Mick persisted. Tom continued to stare at the single twenty on the floor as if expecting it to grow. Mick tossed two more twenties beside the first.

"There was a man, one of our regulars, who stopped to talk with her. I think that they left together." He trailed off indicating that there was more to the story if only he had more cash to lubricate his mind.

"Got a name?" Mick patiently asked. He tossed five more twenties on the pile.

"Rodger Johnson. He's some sort of attorney in town. About fiftyish, balding," Tom recalled. Obviously out of information, he bent down to pick up his cash. As his head came forward and down, it ran into Mick's fist which was coming up. His head snapped up, and he reached for his nose. Mick expertly kicked upward into Tom's crotch which caused him to reflexly bend forward again while holding his privates. Mick moved around behind him and pushed his butt hard with his foot, sending Tom crashing headfirst into the weight stack. He slumped to the floor bleeding from his head and his nose but never let go of his groin area. Mick picked up the loose cash and put it back into his pocket.

Once back on the street, he phoned April Chauncy. "Got some info, April."

"I hope so because I'm getting nothing," she said.

"We are looking for a lawyer named Rodger Johnson who left with our girl. Can your people run this down?" Mick asked.

"I'll get them right on it and let you know. Meet for lunch?" she said.

Mutt & Jeff's Grill
1130 hours

"Gee, April, I sort of feel overdressed in this place," Mick said looking around. The place was crowded but a bit seedy, and the floor and tables were dirty. Mick brushed the food crumbs off the table with a napkin and sat down.

"Yes, it's a bit on the downside. The clientele is mostly law enforcement or lawyers. We might get some information on this Johnson fellow here," April said in a low voice.

They looked over the thumb-worn menus in silence. April's phone went off, and she picked it up and listened intently. After she hung up, she said,

"We have to go. They just found Johnson's body in his apartment. Looks like we are after a bad girl after all."

Rodger Johnson's Apartment, Seattle
1215 hours

The body was lying face down on the living room floor. The apartment was in a high-rise near the water with an impressive view. The furniture was dark, lacquered wood in the Chinese style and highly decorated. The plush rug had once been snow white but now had an ugly dark red stain spreading from the head wound of the body lying on it. After Agent Chauncy showed her credentials, the police present deferred to her.

"Let's turn him over," she requested and two officers carefully rolled him to his back. There was a small caliber entry wound in the forehead. "Mick, perhaps your Sasha killed her driver. Same M.O. She turned around and said in a loud voice, "Search the floor carefully and try to find a 22 shell casing."

"We did that already, Agent Chauncy. We didn't find anything."

"Special Agent Chauncy, Officer," she corrected.

"Excuse me, ma'am," the officer said.

Mick edged past the policemen and bent down for a closer look at the victim's bare feet. After a moment, he stood and motioned for April to look at something. When she came over, he said, "This man has been tortured before being shot. Look at the restraint marks around the ankles and then look carefully at his great toe nails. She could see several thin red lines which appeared to be under the nails, and there was a minute amount of blood at the end of the toe. "Yes, I see what you mean. This puts a different slant on things," she said.

"Somehow, the Russians got here before us. They tortured the man to find out what happened to Sasha and then killed him so he couldn't tell us anything. They don't want us to find her. She is on the run for real and running for her life," Mick said.

"What created the marks on the toes?"

"It's a kit they carry. They push two small electrodes under the toenails, which is bad enough, then they apply a high voltage current until the prisoner talks. They usually do, and quickly."

April stood and waved one the uniformed officers over. "Check the DMV and find out what kind of car Johnson had and put out an APB on it. Did you find his wallet in the apartment?".

"The wallet is over there. Still has his ID but no credit cards or money. We couldn't find any car keys anywhere. By the way, there are dirty dishes and glasses in the kitchen. The suspect may have been here at least several hours," the officer noted.

"Print everything," April said. "We want to know everyone who was here."

"I have to go back to question a source, April. I overlooked asking him something," Mick said. She nodded to him as he left. Mick had to make sure that the little Russian spy wasn't craftily faking being chased. She still might be the killer of both men, he realized. He needed to confirm that someone was chasing her and not be swayed by the physical evidence.

The same young lady was at the desk, and this time didn't smile at him.

"Tom Spelling still here?" Mick asked.

"You should know that he isn't," she answered curtly. "You made a bad enemy this time. Tom is an awfully rough fellow, and when he left, he said that he was going to get you if it was the last thing he did."

"I hurt his pride. I would like to apologize to him, and I need you to give me his address," Mick said with a smile.

This time she grinned. "It's your funeral, but if I were you, I would stay far away from him." She proceeded to flip through her files and wrote Tom's address down and gave it to him. "One more thing, whomever you are, you better hope that Tom's biker buddies aren't around when you see him."

"Thanks, dear, and thanks for the advice," Mick said as he turned to leave.

Roy Street, Seattle

Mick parked about a block from the address and walked so that he could get a feel of the neighborhood. This part of town was definitely in decline, with trash accumulation on the street and the side alleys and graffiti in shades of red and blue on the walls. The building he was walking toward was a wood-framed two-story, and there were several large chopper and hog-style motorcycles parked outside. Mick checked the address, confirming that this was the place. He climbed the short set of stairs and knocked hard at the door.

After a moment, the door jerked open and the mountainous shadow of Tom Spelling filled the frame. Mick could hear some deep voices coming around him from inside the house.

"Well, as I live and breathe," Tom said. "Hey, guys, it's the jerk who broke my nose this morning, standing right here in front of me." There was some scuffling and the bearded faces of three large men appeared in front of Tom. One of them showed a gap-toothed smile with an isolated gold tooth. A couple of others with nearly identical facial hair looked from the other side. "What the hell do you think is going to happen to you coming here, stupid?" Tom asked.

"The way I see it, Tom, if you just answer a couple of simple questions, you don't have to have any more parts broken," Mick said very slowly as if Tom were an idiot.

"That's it!" Tom shouted in anger. "Beat this little shit until he is red meat!" he screamed and partially moved out of the way. Mick stepped back one step to allow room and waited with his arms at his sides. The first one to come through the door was the one with the gold-tooth. He was nearly as large as Tom, wearing a dirty jeans-style vest and black shirt, and beaming with anticipation of beating on Mick. As he reached out, there was a sudden fast motion from Mick, and the side of his 45 slapped the man in the lower face, sending a bloody gold tooth skidding across the floor. An arc of blood spewed from his split lips, and the man fell forward off the porch onto the sidewalk. Mick leveled the pistol at Tom's head and moved toward the door. He pushed Tom hard in the chest backing him up to make enough room to enter.

When he was fully in the room, he said, "I don't have a problem shooting all of you, but you have a choice here. Just answer a couple of questions, and I'll leave you alone." The gun in Mick's hand exploded at a table lamp which flew apart in a shower of glass. Mick put his left hand around Tom's throat, pointing his pistol at the other two, who backed up against the wall together, anger radiant on their faces. Tom was making choking sounds but didn't dare try to grab Mick's hand or arm.

"First question, Tom," Mick said. "Did anyone else ask about the girl before I did? By the way, if you lie to me, I'll kill you right now." The voice he used was chilling, even to these men used to a violent life. Their instincts told them that Mick was a man to be feared and a man who meant what he said.

"Yes," Tom croaked. He raised up on his toes to try to lessen pressure on his throat.

"Next question," Mick said and tightened his grip on Tom's throat and pushed him higher. "Did the man or men have a Russian accent?"

"Shit, man," Tom sputtered. "I don't know Russian. They were foreign. That's all I know. Don't kill me, man," Tom begged. Mick hooked his left leg behind Tom's and pushed hard against his throat sending him crashing to the floor on his back. The house shook. He continued to glare at the men against the wall. "Don't give me a reason to hurt you boys, and you will be happier in the long run," Mick informed them. "Now, if anyone comes outside after I leave, he will catch a bullet. Understand?" There was no response to his question. He pushed open the door with his foot and backed out onto the small porch. A glance found the first man propped up against the building, his hands holding his face. Blood was seeping around his fingers and trickling down both arms. Mick moved sideways out of the doorframe and waited, his pistol pointed at the door opening. After some low angry voices were heard, the profile of one of the men emerged from the door. Mick swung the pistol in an arc landing a solid blow at the junction of his nose and forehead, causing him to fall straight backward, leaving his large feet sticking out of the door. "I warned you. Next one out dies," Mick said. He turned and slowly walked away. No one else came out of the door.

Mick drove slowly away and dialed April. "Hi. There were Russians on her trail, and they got there before us. We have to find her before they do. Any luck on the getaway car?"

"He had a late model Lexus. We have an APB out on the car, but we have to wait on results. It may take days to find it."

"What about tracers on any credit cards he carried?"

"I have people who are looking through Johnson's papers right now to find his credit card numbers. They will finish soon and then we'll have the FBI put a watch on any activity. Ready for lunch yet?"

"You know, I've worked up quite an appetite since I left you. Could we go upscale a bit with the next place? You know, I don't dress up very often, and I have to make good use of it."

Top of The Hilton
1600 hours

The smartly-dressed waiter popped the cork on the wine bottle and offered the cork to Mick. He raised his eyebrows when Mick ignored him and so he poured a small amount into a glass and slid it across the linen toward him.

"You are supposed to taste it to see if the wine meets your approval," April said, grinning at his discomfort. She had exchanged her sweatshirt for a silk blouse which revealed a necklace dangling a small white stone which showered the room with small points of color.

Mick hesitantly sipped the offered wine and shrugged. The waiter sighed and poured two glasses half-full and slid the wine bottle back in the ice bucket. To Mick's embarrassment, April put her hands to her mouth, suppressing her laugh, while her eyes sparkled with merriment.

"April, I'm doing the best I can," he said in a low voice. "I feel underdressed in this place, and especially with someone who turns every male head within blocks."

"I'm sorry, Mick," she said, still suppressing a laugh. "It's just funny! By the way, casual is the new dressed up. Don't worry about it and just be yourself." Her phone buzzed in silent mode, and she frowned, reluctantly picking it up. "Special Agent Chauncy." Mick could hear the small tinny voice on the other end but couldn't make out any words. He watched her face for expression change but saw little. She hung up and looked at Mick as if thinking about what she was going to say. He patiently waited for her, until finally she spoke, "Interesting. We have a trace on Johnson's credit card activity and already have four hits. Two are for gas and included fast food. Two are for clothes. She is on Interstate 5 heading south. The last one was in Sacramento, so she is driving through the night. The bad news? The Lexus was found in Salem so she has switched cars. So far, no reports of more dead guys with missing cars."

"There is not much for us to do yet," Mick said and drifted off in thought. "I see something interesting, though." He had April's attention, and she put down her wine glass. "She is a well-trained Russian agent, but she is using credit cards that she knows will be traced. She isn't using the back roads, but the Interstate. She has changed cars who knows how many times. The point is that she wants us to track her but not catch her. She would know that her Russian friends will track her also but not as fast as we will. I think that she is giving us a heads-up, hoping we will find the bad guys who are trying to find her."

April nodded understanding and then wondered, "A very dangerous game. Why doesn't she just defect to us?"

"This isn't the Cold War any longer, even though it is. If she comes in to us, the Russians will present evidence proving that she is a murderer and also a rogue. She could end up either going to prison in the U.S. or, worse, handed over to them. Best solution for her would be to have help from the CIA to stay free in return for working for us."

April smiled again, "And the best possible person to find her and help her out is....wait for it....Mick Grundy! Don't you see that she is still trying to get you on her side? She is still trying to recruit you for something."

"April, how would she know that I would be the one to find her? The evidence points to her actually fleeing her former Russian bosses. We have no real reason to suspect more complex motives."

"Two very good reasons, Mick. The first is woman's intuition. Mine. The second is that these are Russians we are dealing with, and you would know better than anyone that you can't believe what you think you see."

They stopped talking about the case and enjoyed the evening. The view from the top of the Hilton was impressive, and the food excellent. Mick had never experienced a single upscale evening out. He intended to when things settled down with Anna, but she died before he could get the chance. All of his adult life had been in the service of his country, either in the elite units of the Army Special Forces or in the employment of the CIA. It had been a constant life of danger and violence, and he could no longer dream of an end and something on the other side.

April beamed at him from across the table in the low-level warm light. "Mick, I have never been so wrong about someone as I was about you. I just didn't understand, and I am sorry for it."

"Don't say that, April. It's just what you thought. I am a highly skilled brute whose first reflex is to shoot to kill. I have no cultural skills, no refinements and little joy within me. That is so in contrast with you who appears to be both physically beautiful and highly intelligent as well as refined. We are a real pair, aren't we?"

"Just remember that we are partners, Mick. We act in concert, each using our particular gifts to accomplish our mission."

Mick smiled back at her while studying her face and eyes. "I have to get used to it, April. Mostly, I have worked alone. You have to keep tugging on my sleeve to remind me."

"By the way, you have to pay for tonight. My FBI budget hacks will turn purple if this meal shows up on my expense account!"

Tok-A-Lou Avenue
2200 hours

Mick opened the front door very softly. The living room lights were on, but he wasn't sure that Jennifer had retired or was waiting up for him. As he turned the corner from the hall, he saw her sitting on the couch, a book in her hand. As soon as she saw him, she stood and ran toward him.

"I always worry about you, Mick. You were gone for hours!" she said and wrapped her arms around him. "Can you tell me what you did today?"

"Not completely, Jennifer. I have been asked to work on a case with an FBI agent, and we started early today. Thanks again for the loan of the clothes and the car. I felt human again for a while," Mick said and returned her embrace.

"Your new partner, is she pretty?" Jennifer asked in a small voice.

"Jennifer, she is only a partner, not a lover. Besides, you are a unique person, full of life and personality. You are fun to be with and lovely to look at. You are not in competition with any woman in my eyes," Mick said into the top of her head.

Jennifer squeezed harder. "Please don't tell me you are leaving, Mick. We haven't had a chance to convince you to stay with us, and what will I tell Jonnie?

Mick held on, rocking her back and forth, resting his chin on her head. " Some high-level people asked that I take this case. I am the only one who has seen this person, and in some way, it relates and comes back to me. There is no choice, I have to take it, Jennifer. My future, our future, may depend on what happens and what I find. There may be some chance that I won't be hunted any longer, but if nothing changes, I couldn't live with myself if my problems caused either one of you harm."

They stood there that way for a long time, lost in thought and, at least for the moment, safe in each other's arms.

United Flight 457 Somewhere Over California
0745 hours

They were touching shoulders, sitting side by side. Mick found it delightful to travel right out in the open and not by stealth. He watched as Special Agent Chauncy flashed her badge or her smile to get what she wanted from people. They were efficiently whisked into the plane, bypassing security or scanners, and she even had the seating assignments of two passengers changed to allow her and Mick to sit together. She opened her briefcase with a snap and took out some papers.

"Our girl is leading us right to Vegas, and we should get there nearly the same time. At least, there were no more dead men on the trail, only drunken ones. She is using the Johnson credit cards instead of the new ones, and we are letting the charges go through. It's an obvious, wide and neon-lit trail, and it will be interesting to see where she goes in Vegas and for what reason she headed there." April summarized.

Mick looked into the distance over her shoulder while thinking it through. "Well, she has a new wardrobe now and cash to spend, and there are places in Vegas which are not very discrete concerning who stays as long as there is money. She will hook up again with a man is my guess. She seems to be able to do it whenever she wants."

"We have issued her photo to all the big casinos. They all have very good surveillance systems, and some of them use automated facial recognition. If she goes anywhere near there, they will contact us."

"Do you have an opinion as to whether the GRU has access to the same information?"

"Money talks," April answered.

76

Chapter 7

Linkage

Caesars Palace
1430 hours

Mick lifted the brown paper wrapped package left in the seat after the man got up, tucked it into a small shopping bag that he unfolded and got up to leave. The entire drop only took two minutes to execute. Zeskie always came through, Mick mused to himself. He had placed the call from the airport after they arrived that morning, while he was in the restroom. Zeskie had only taken five minutes to call back with a location for the pick up. The delivery was scheduled for the afternoon using the lobby of Caesars Palace. The package would include a new identity, or even several, complete with history and photos, also money and an untraceable credit card issued to one of the fake aliases. The weight of the package also told him that there was another 45 caliber pistol and ammo. He walked unhurriedly toward one of the service doors and waited until someone passed through. He slipped inside after one of the workers passed by him. In the dark corridor, he opened the package and distributed the contents into his pockets. He replaced the gun he carried with the new one and carefully wiped the old one down, removing his fingerprints, afterward dropping it into a nearby trash bin. He walked back outside into the oven-heat of southern Nevada and blended with the crowds crossing an overpass over Las Vegas Boulevard. They were staying in adjoining rooms in the Venetian, directly across the street. April had taken off to meet with several local FBI agents and fill them in on the case. She and Mick were scheduled to meet in her room before dinner to plan and to review any new facts. Mick took his time and strolled around, taking in the sights and gawking at the disparate display of humanity visiting and working in Vegas. Once before, he had been here on a case but not long enough to see anything. He had found his man quickly and shot him in the chest while they were riding the Monorail. After the killing, he had made a quick exit from Vegas in the middle of the night, engineered by the unflappable Zeskie. There was no way to be sure if they were right about Sasha coming to Vegas; all they could do at the moment is to sit tight and wait. If she showed, however, there could be a fast-paced series of events and no way of predicting how it would go.

Mick picked up a drink from a cute cocktail waitress and lounged on a stool in front of a row of chiming slot machines. He studied the camera surveillance pods in the ceiling and along the corridors. They were watching everyone, and if Sasha walked into one of these places, she would be rapidly identified. He could see the casino's main entrance between two machines, and as he casually looked around, he noticed two men in dark suits walk in. There was something about them that made Mick start watching more closely. Both were burly in a fat but strong kind of way and both had wandering eyes. They were looking for someone, and they moved back to one side of the flow of people and stood there without talking, continuing to scan the crowd. One of them put his hand to his ear, a dead giveaway of a communication device. Mick started to feel more uneasy about the men and furtively looked around for others like them. He decided to dial April.

"Hi, Mick," she answered brightly. "Are you waiting for me?"

"Do you have any agents down here at the Venetian casino right now?" And, by the way, do your guys come in pairs with dark suits?"

April paused. "Our guys haven't dressed like that for years, and I didn't hear about any operations in that casino. What are they doing?"

"They are watching the entrance. I can't see the other entry or exit doors from here, so I don't know if they are alone, but I am getting some bad vibes about it." As he spoke, a young man dressed in the purple jacket of the casino staff came up to one of the men and whispered something in his ear, then turned and pointed to Mick's location. The man in the suit put something in the boy's hand, and he and his companion started walking in Mick's direction. "Listen, April, they are coming my way. I have to try to avoid them in case I am the target. If it's not me they are after, I'll meet you in your room as planned, but if I am the one they came for, I'll have to go underground and contact you later."

"Wait there, Mick, we are coming!" she shouted, but then realized that the phone had lost its connection. Putting the phone down, she stood, pointing at the three FBI agents with her. "Get your gear, we have to go NOW," and she started checking her weapon.

"Where are we headed?" one of them asked.

"To the Venetian. I think Mick Grundy has been spotted, and they will kill him if they get close. Someone call Casino Security, and let them know to shut down the exits until we get there." They all left together while pulling on their jackets emblazoned with FBI in large letters. The two older agents picked up submachine guns on their way out, and they all took off at a run for the car. "How long till we get there?" April asked.

"Thirty...forty-five, 'pends on traffic," one of them answered.

April started biting her lower lip. She knew that Mick was experienced and would not hesitate to shoot if provoked, but there were just too many unknowns to figure what could happen. Hopefully, this was a false alarm, and no one had actually spotted him. Could be though, that this is what she had feared all along. The operative, Sasha, whom they were tracking, could actually be bait, not a fugitive. She left a clear trail and obviously wanted Mick to show up where he could be the one spotted. The crowds in Vegas make a perfect killing ground, because a killer can get close without being noticed.

They might have him boxed in with men at every exit.

Mick eased out of his chair and walked away toward one of the rear exits which led toward the Monorail stop. He joined a small crowd of steady walkers, and they all moved like a living snake along the carpeted path. Ahead, Mick could see two more, nearly identical men, standing on either side of the exit door and watching the crowd. He knew that they could see him, if he could see them. He took a quick right along a small corridor which connected to one of the shopping areas. The path turned sharply right, and he could see the other side of the casino area at the end of the hall. There were several closed metal doors which were unmarked. He tried each as he passed and discovered one which opened. He went through and found himself at the head of a small concrete staircase headed down with another metal door at the bottom. He quickly descended and as the lower door was closing behind him, he heard the first door open with a click. Someone was right behind him. Mick went to one side of the door and drew his weapon. He could hear muffled conversation and more than one set of footsteps on the stairs.

The door opened slowly as if the person was wary of what could be on the other side. From the back side of the door, Mick could see a large head emerge, looking both ways. A silencer, followed by the barrel of the gun, crept into view. A dark suit sleeve followed as the man came cautiously across the threshold. A voice from the rear said, *"Вы видите его?"* ["Do you see him?"]

"Yes, you see him," Mick said and fired at the man's temporal area. As the man fell away, Mick leaned around the open door and opened fire at the man's companion, hitting him in the head. As the explosions from Mick's 45 reverberated around the concrete walls, he held his position, waiting for anyone else coming through the door. He reached down to the first fallen man and pulled his earpiece off and put it into his own ear. The device was made to both hear and talk.

A tinny voice said, *"Вы находили Большое жюри?"* ["Did you find Grundy?"] into his ear.

Mick answered, *"Подошедший быстро. Мы ранили его и заманились в ловушку его."* ["Come here quickly. We have wounded him and have him trapped."]

"Мы находимся на пути. Пребывание там." ["We are on the way. Stay there."] Mick smiled at their eagerness to die. He pulled the bodies from the staircase so that the door would again close. Soon, he could hear the upper door open and more footsteps on the stairs.

"В здесь. Мы имеем его." ["In here. We have him."] Mick said.

The door opened and Mick stepped around it and opened fire. Two more bodies fell down the stairs and were pulled into the room. Mick closed the door and waited. *"Торопитесь, мы нуждаемся в большем количестве помощи!"* ["Hurry, we need more help!"] Mick announced.

A different voice in his ear said, *"Вы - самостоятельно. Слишком много полицейских здесь теперь. Удача."* ["You are on your own. Too many police here now. Good luck."]

Mick called April on his black phone. "Hi," he said when she answered.

"Mick, we are here looking for you. Where are you, and are you all right?" April asked, speaking rapidly.

"I'm fine. I'll meet you in the casino area in just a moment. Better look out for some bad guys up there."

He carefully wiped his pistol down and threw it on the chest of one of the bodies. Retrieving a gun from the dead man's hand, he slid it into the holster in the small of his own back. As he was walking down the corridor toward the casino, he could hear April's voice loudly giving instructions. He came into the large room and leaned into a column, looking appreciatively at her and watching her work from a distance. She was wearing a white blouse, a dark skirt and was clearly in command. When she looked in his direction, he gave her a thumbs up and waved her over, then put his index finger to his lips to let her know to not point him out. She nodded understanding, then leaned over to one of her male companions and said something to him. She started walking toward Mick and couldn't resist giving him a smile in return. He turned before she arrived and led her away into a quiet corner.

"Did your people round up any suspects?"

"Good to see that you are all right, Mick. First you get to tell me if you found any bad guys or if they found you instead."

"Yeah, I ran into some and solved their problem for them. It's important, April. Did you capture any?"

"We rounded up everybody who looked or acted in the slightest way suspicious, and they are being processed now. I don't know yet if any of them were after you."

"Look for Russians," Mick suggested. "It's not too hard."

"Well, Mick, guess we can't stay in the Venetian tonight."

"Now do you see why I was sleeping in the lion's cage?" he asked. "I should get out of here before they find the bodies."

"Bodies? Plural?" Her eyebrows went up.

Mick didn't answer knowing that the facts would soon make everything obvious. "Say, isn't your team still here and will be here for some time?"

"Yes, we have a lot of work to do to try to understand how the Russians were so organized, and we have an angry crowd who have to be interviewed and either dismissed or arrested."

"Let's go up to the 'Eye in the Sky' room and find out how they found me, and why they turned me over to the Russians." He put his hand on her shoulder to convince her to go with him. They cornered a floor manager and inquired about the location of the security offices and headed that way. April identified herself while holding her badge in the face of a guard, who gladly opened the door to the nerve center of the big casino.

"I need to talk to the manager," April announced loudly, and the room became quiet. A portly man walked forward and identified himself as the Chief Security Officer.

The man looked carefully at her badge before asking, "How can we help you, Agent Chauncy?"

"Special Agent Chauncy, Mr. Bennet,' she corrected.

"Pardon me, Special Agent," he bristled a bit.

"Someone in this room has been subverted by a foreign agency, and if I don't get quick and truthful answers, I will arrest everyone in this room until the matter is cleared," she said loudly, using an aggressive tone.

Mr. Bennet glanced from the face of Special Agent Chauncy to Mick. He seemed to recognize Mick and shuddered slightly at seeing his angry face up close, stuttering, "Let's discuss this in my office, Special Agent, if you please."

"No, we won't, Mr. Bennet. You are under arrest, turn around and put your arms behind you. We will discuss this in *my* office." She surveyed all the faces looking toward her, instead of their monitors. "All of you, listen up. You will stand up and move away from your workstations and remain in that position until the Swat Team arrives."

Bennet complied and put his hands behind him, but protested, "Special Agent, please, let me explain. It wasn't our fault. Please listen. Your actions could cost the casino millions of dollars. Please!" April was in no mood for compromise, and she whipped out a pair of handcuffs and snapped them in place, then forcefully turned Bennet around to face her.

"Talk, and it better be convincing," she said, leaning toward his face.

Two days ago, we had a visit such as yours from

individuals who identified themselves as the FBI. They had credentials and badges and a court order requiring us to comply with assisting them. They supplied digital photos of this man beside you, and we were instructed to call them if he was discovered on our property. We just did as they ordered. Don't you people talk to each other? There should be records somewhere backing up what happened."

"You big fat dumb ass. They were Russians from the GRU. This man you identified could have been killed today. The Russians certainly tried. I should put you in prison for being stupid. Being a traitor isn't enough." She was angry and seemed to rise up on her toes while she leaned toward him. There wasn't a sound in the room as all the security people were listening closely. April continued after catching her breath, "What about the face of the girl, Sasha, who you were supposed to look for? I personally called here yesterday about finding her. Did you bother to look for her or not?"

"Yes, Special Agent, we were looking, but the other agents insisted that we call them directly, if we found her."

"Well, did you find her or not?" April screamed into his face.

"Well, yes, Special Agent. We spotted her last night, and we called the number the FBI agents gave us, as ordered," Bennet said. He had begun to sweat and tremble.

Mick interrupted, "I want to see the tape with her on it. Right now."

At the sound of Mick's voice, Bennet started visibly

shaking. He nodded toward one of the older men on the end of the aisle, "JoJo, please show them anything they want."

They left Bennet standing in the middle of the floor and moved over to JoJo's desk. He spun some dials and clicked his keyboard and soon the image of Sasha was seen entering the casino gambling area. She walked with seeming purpose toward one of the tables and stood there looking around, apparently waiting on something or someone, and looking directly at the camera once or twice. She was dressed in evening wear and glitter was flashing from her wrist and neck. After a cocktail waitress put a drink in her hand, she turned and leaned over one of the tables, far enough to emphasize her attractive rear end. The sight of her moving buttocks was enough to entice a young man who came up to her and started a conversation. The scene was captured on three different cameras, each from a different angle. She seemed to size him up as inadequate for her needs and dismissed him with wave her hand, then went back to displaying her butt. It didn't take long and another, better dressed man, was attracted to her. This time she approved and constantly made eyes at him and, occasionally, caressed his chest with delicate feminine gestures. The two walked together arm in arm and slowly left the casino.

Mick asked JoJo, "Can you identify the second man?"

JoJo clicked away for a while and then said, "No. He is not in our records. Sorry."

"I know that the casinos cooperate and share

information. You are directed to share this man's photo with all of them and ask them to send the FBI anything they have about him," April ordered. JoJo nodded and proceeded to click away at his terminal, sending the request out. Two agents appeared at the door armed with black, menacing submachine guns. April tugged Mick's sleeve, and they headed out past the new arrivals. April leaned over to one of them and whispered, "Hold them here for a couple of hours, then let them go."

The other agent followed them out the door and said, "Special Agent Chauncy, do you want the local police to remove the four bodies from downstairs, or is there some reason for us to take them in?"

"Four bodies?" she asked while looking at Mick. "Have them sent to the Clark County Crime Lab, and we'll be watching closely as they go over them." The agent picked up his phone to give instructions as they started to walk away. Mick pulled out the gun he had picked from the first assassin and handed it to April, butt first.

"I picked this off the first one down. You might find that it matches the slugs in the driver and Johnson. If it does, it means that Sasha is not the shooter and is really on the run as she appears."

April took the gun and turned it over a couple of times. "American made except for the silencer. No serial number either. Could be the gun, but Mick, there is another possibility you need to consider." Mick raised his eyebrows waiting for the other shoe. "Don't you see that they set this whole thing up in advance. Sasha is part of a team. She leads, and they follow in a moving trap specifically designed to get you. You are the target. Forget the ES she handed you about some internal conspiracy. I think that you should give up the chase for her. You might be unlucky enough to find her."

Mick shrugged, "I won't know until I see her in the flesh. Remember, we were given this assignment; I didn't ask for it. Anyway, I'm hungry, let's eat."

Chapter 8

Contact

Eiffel Tower Restaurant, Las Vegas
1915 hours

They were seated against the outside window in a table for two, complete with candles. Across the street, the fountains and lights of the hourly show from the Bellagio were exploding and dancing across the water. Mick leaned across the table and asked April, "Would it be acceptable if we also ordered a drink before dinner?"

April giggled a bit and said, "That is very appropriate, Mick, and it lets us celebrate the fact that you escaped harm once more. By the way, my agents and I talked it over, and we think if the FBI had been delayed a little longer, you would have killed them all and saved us a lot of work."

Mick answered without looking up, "I am very happy that you arrived when you did, and please, hold the catsup and the sarcasm." Their waiter, who arrived in a splendid and flawless starched white uniform stood waiting patiently for an order. Mick motioned him closer, then speaking in perfect Parisian French asked, *"Je suppose que vous parlez le français dans un restaurant français?"*

The waiter looked a bit shocked but quickly recovered and answered, *"Monsieur, vous parlez le français excellent. Je serais heureux de recevoir votre ordre aussi dans le français."*

Mick nodded knowingly, as if their conversation was a closely guarded secret and very private. *"Parfait. Nous aurons deux martini sec et hors-d'oeuvre d'escargots et de pain français."* The waiter smiled approval and briskly left to retrieve the order.

April had her mouth open in surprise. "I knew that you had some language skills, but I had no idea of how versatile you could be. You even looked French when you were speaking. By the way, what did you order?"

"Surprise, April, I have some skills other than killing," Mick answered, smiling at her as if he had scored a triumph. "One thing that I want to describe to you is my delight when you were angry at the director of hotel security earlier. Your nostrils flared, your face colored, and your eyes dilated. You had the man ready to puke with fear."

"Seems that I'm not plastic after all, doesn't it?" She still wore her white blouse from earlier in the morning, but seen by candlelight and against the backdrop of the captivating water fireworks, she was magnetic, even enchanting. The waiter brought the drinks, laid the napkins across their laps and fussed with the arrangement of the silverware. He kept giving sidelong looks at April and seemed hesitant to leave. When finally he did, April asked, "What is his problem? Do I have egg on my face, or something?"

Mick whispered, "I would think that you would be used to it by now. Isn't it obvious that he doesn't see a woman as beautiful as you very often? Possibly never?"

April took it in without comment. She was used to it, after all. "Was your wife, Anna, beautiful, Mick?"

It took a long time for him to answer. "She was my whole life, my everything. I thought that she was the most lovely woman in the world when I was with her."

"Do you often still think of her?"

"I was at her side at the moment of her death. She was trying to speak to me, but I couldn't hear her. The same memory comes back to me every night since that day, and I always wake up with a racing pulse and soaked in sweat. I try to dream about the good times, but it always gets back to that last minute of her life."

April thought this over and was unable to offer anything of comfort. "Perhaps when you find someone else to love, it might help."

"That thought has crossed my mind. I have to be sure that I won't bring the same danger to another person I love. Right now, I am still hunted, and it isn't the time for me to have a close personal relationship with a woman. It could cost her life, and it would cost me as well, because I would lose her also." The waiter returned with the appetizer plates and waited patiently for the rest of their order.

"April, I would appreciate some suggestions for dinner, and your choice of wine," Mick urged. She considered her preferences while the waiter waited patiently. The magic of the evening wasn't entirely broken, even though the past had once again been resurrected so vividly. Mick couldn't help but notice the woman across from him. She was not only breathtakingly perfect, but also so very much alive. He had begun to read the occasional flickers of temperament pass over her as he understood her better and as he studied her, he realized that her emotions and thoughts were to be found in the depths of her eyes, not on her face. They had developed a very strong bond in only a few days, and they were becoming friends as well as partners.

Mick's phone rang, and he reluctantly picked it up. "Zeskie here, Mick," the voice said. "I gather that you and your new partner are developing into a team. Much better than antagonism, isn't it?" he chuckled.

"This isn't a good time, Zeskie, for small talk. Is there something of importance you need to say?" While he was listening to Zeskie, he noticed that April was talking into her phone.

Zeskie answered, "I heard about the shootings in the Venetian. Glad you are all right, and I'll be sending you another package tomorrow. Same place, same messenger. By the way, we are getting more noise from our listening stations about problems in the GRU. There were a couple of defections yesterday, and they told the same story. We would like to talk to this girl you are chasing, if you can catch her, that is. Try not to get killed in the process, will you?"

"I'm sitting across from Special Agent Chauncy right now, and she feels strongly that Sasha is bait to catch me and that we are following a moving trap. What are your feelings?"

"I respect your partner, or I wouldn't have paired you two. She may be right, but it doesn't matter. If Sasha is actually running, she will have to work with us if we get our hands on her. But if she is part of a trap, we must catch her to shut down her network. We'll squeeze her dry of information, if you can manage to bring her back alive. My advice is to pursue and get her. By the way, is the food good there at the Vegas Eiffel Tower, or is the view you have so good that it makes up for it?"

Before Mick answered, he looked over at April who was still engaged in conversation on her phone. He watched the light play on her glossy lips as she spoke, her eyebrows moving with her mood, the swell of her chest as she breathed, the candlelight glittering from her shiny hair. Behind her, the fountains of the Bellagio danced in colored lights. "Zeskie, the view from here is worth the trip."

He sat in silence as she finished her conversation. The waiter was a few feet away, still patiently waiting for their order, and moved toward the table. April held her open hand up to stop him. She leaned toward Mick and said quietly, "She has been seen not far from here. We have to go."

Mick threw a crisp hundred on the table and shrugged in a French way at the waiter as they left. He wrapped his arm under hers and pulled her closer. "What gives?" he asked.

"Five minutes ago, Hotel Security in the Bellagio across the street spotted her in their sports bar. She was alone and sitting on a bar stool," she said under her breath as they rode the elevator down to the casino floor. As they stepped off, Mick noticed a couple of FBI jackets in the distance. At least they were still in this casino, but across the street was a different matter. Mick, by habit, checked for the gun at his back and then remembered that he had left it at the shooting scene. The other pistol had been given to April earlier to be examined by the crime lab. He was unarmed, except for a pocket knife. Not much value in a shooting situation.

April stopped to get his attention, "Another thing you need to know. There have been no fingerprints left by this girl from anyplace we know she has been. She's carefully wiping down anything she touches. All we have to go on is photographs, and your memory of what she looks like. By the way, preliminary testing on the gun you recovered is positive for the prior shootings, and the dead guys in the Venetian all had fake, but excellent, reproductions of FBI badges." She shook his arm until he looked directly at her. "You know that there were some that got away, right? They could be over there waiting for you right now. We don't have to go looking for her. I could get the place shut as tight as a coffin first." Mick studied her but didn't respond, and they resumed walking forward. "Mick, I'm asking you not to go. Do it for me, will you?" She had tears in her eyes and pleading in her face.

Mick gently wiped away a tear from her cheek. "You know that they have more to fear from me than I do from them. My reputation throws them off balance. We have to do this before she can get away again, but I want you to drop behind me when we get close. You can avoid fire that way and also protect my back."

Vegas never closes, and the hours before midnight are especially busy. A determined walker with a little luck with crowds will take a full thirty minutes to cross over Las Vegas Boulevard and walk around the lake to enter the palatial Bellagio. The best Mick and April could do was to follow the ambling crowd. April made contact with her agents over the phone as they walked and instructed them to quickly and silently take up stations around the casino area. She was informed that Sasha was still hanging around the sports bar but had attracted male admirers and could leave at any time. When they entered, April made eye contact with a plainclothes agent already in place by the door. He nodded subtly to her and, by a twitch of his head, indicated that other agents were already inside. As instructed, April lagged behind Mick farther and farther as they walked toward the back of the casino and the sports bar. Mick carefully stayed with the crowd to blend in. Over their heads, he located the far end of the casino and made his way along the side wall, past the cashier's cages.

There she was, brazenly sitting with crossed legs on a stool at the end of the bar while she and two attentive men engaged in conversation. Mick glanced around but could see no obvious threats nearby and casually walked toward them. The woman was indeed Sasha, and she noticed him without showing any surprise, continuing her flirting with both men. One of them spun around angrily to Mick and hissed, "Four is a crowd. Take off, Bub. We saw her first." While keeping eye contact with Sasha, Mick methodically reached down and found the man's groin with his hand, then grabbed and squeezed hard. The man fell like a stone to the floor, breathless and clutching his privates with his two hands. The other man slowly backed away leaving Mick and Sasha face to face.

"I've been waiting for you, Mick," she said with sleepy eyes. She was wearing heavy makeup with lavish green eye shadow which matched her green eyes. Mick scanned her figure, clearly visible through her low cut, clinging silk dress. Her long brown hair spilled over her shoulder, setting off the white of her elegant neck. She was the perfection of sex appeal, complete with curves and languid body language. No wonder she could find a man at the snap of her fingers, Mick thought. The fellow on the floor started to groan, and Mick noticed movement in his peripheral vision; someone was coming to investigate a disturbance.

"Have you trapped me, Sasha, or have I captured you?" Mick asked. She smiled and eased off the stool with catlike fluidity and stood before him, face to face.

"They only let me live so that they could get us both. I tried to run and leave you clues, but I couldn't get away. I knew that your people would find me in one of these places, but our enemies are here also and are somewhere close, keeping me in view. I have the feeling of eyes on me. There is no hope for me, but if you are quick, you might still get away. Run, Mick."

A heavily-built man in a suit approached them from the side. Mick turned to get a good look, and he saw the hard eyes and face of an experienced ex-policeman working security for the casino. Judging by his appearance, he was sure to be carrying a weapon. He came up cautiously, stepping around the one on the floor writhing in pain and clutching his groin. Mick could tell that the newcomer was sizing him up to gauge any threat before speaking.

"What happened here?" he asked in a demanding voice. Mick could see over the security man's shoulder; others were also coming toward him. Two husky men in poor fitting suits were spreading out, and they had their eyes fixed on him. Mick didn't answer the security man as the other men ominously converged toward them behind his back. As he expected, one of the men drew a pistol as he came near. Mick suddenly moved into the security officer, reaching under his suit coat for the gun he knew would be hanging under his left arm. The gun was there, and Mick drew it as he pushed the security man backwards to keep him off balance. The Russian coming toward him never saw Mick's gun before it fired through the back of the security man's suit into his oncoming head. Mick pushed away from the security man and flung himself on the floor, sliding partially behind one of the nearby gaming tables, his gun arm on the bottom. At the same moment, a small machine pistol come out of the other assailant's coat. Mick fired two shots between the legs of the table at the man's feet and ankles, making him fall to the floor but still clutching the weapon. Mick got a clear view of the man's rage-filled face just before the gun spewed off the entire magazine of ammo in his direction. Splinters of wood showered the air, the sharp reports of gunfire punctuated by screaming from the panicking gambling crowd. Mick's next shot found the man's head, and the machine gun went silent. The incessant chiming from the slot machines returned as did yet another recording of Sinatra. Mick quickly rose to his feet looking for Sasha, catching sight of her as she fled toward the gathering crowd. Mick started to give chase when he felt himself being spun around by a big hand. The security man had regained his footing and had produced another gun which was pressing into his neck.

"Hold it, Buddy, and drop my gun," the security man commanded.

Mick watched helplessly as Sasha disappeared into the crowd. "Let that man go, right now," April's authoritative voice demanded, and she pushed her FBI badge into the security man's face. He released Mick, who dropped the handgun and bolted in the direction that Sasha had fled.

Two of April's agents wearing the distinctive FBI emblazoned jackets emerged from the crowd and began searching the two bodies lying in spreading stains of blood. One agent stood, holding a folded black wallet similar to his own, "Another set of fake IDs, Special Agent Chauncy," he called out. After he handed April the fake ID, he remarked, "It looks like they were going to assassinate Grundy right here and blame it on us."

"Brazen as hell," April agreed. "They assumed that they could bluff their way out after the shooting using fake ID. Who knows, it might have worked," she added. "Contact the team and see if we can help Grundy catch this girl before she gets away again."

As Mick pushed his way past the crowd of gapers, he tried to catch a glimpse of Sasha. His mind rapidly raced, trying put himself in her position. He realized what he wouldn't do is head for the hotel lobby and entrance. Too obvious. He passed a large corridor just past the elevator bank which headed off to the right, and he made the turn toward a long line of shops. She could blend into any of them as a customer and be hard to spot. He walked with long strides, keeping watch on the stores as he passed. No sign of her ahead in the hall. Just past a gelato cafe, he saw a restroom sign and stopped. He scanned the hall ahead and behind. No threats but also no Sasha. He pushed open the men's door and looked around, then took a deep breath and charged into the ladies' restroom. Two women at the sink looked at him in horror.

"Hotel Security, ladies. Did a young woman dressed in black come in here just now?" Mick asked. One of them hesitantly pointed to a stall with a closed door. Mick rapped softly on the door and said, "It's Mick. The bad guys are down. We can talk now so come on out."

In a moment, the lock snapped open, and the door came ajar far enough for Mick to see her face. She had already put up her hair, trying to change her appearance, and the heavy makeup was gone. The door drifted open, exposing a frightened, hunted animal. Gone was the sultry, sexual being she was moments ago. This woman looked like a child in an adult's world. "I'm not going to hurt you, Sasha," Mick said. She slowly came out of the stall and buried her head in his chest.

"I'm so glad they didn't kill you, Mick. I hope that now you believe me, and we can trust each other. If you can help me get away from here safely, I have a lot of information your people can use."

Mick pushed her away and said, "No, Sasha, I don't trust you. You have yet to earn that. There are FBI agents here who will protect and give you asylum. All we have to do is stay here, and they will come to us."

"I'm no good to you on the inside, Mick. I'll lose my contacts. Most of them are loyal Russians and would view me as a double agent or a spy for the Americans. It would be best if I were free to act as an agent for the group that wants a free Russia. I don't want to betray my motherland, only the corrupt people in control right now. They will try to get me returned by any methods, and you, of all people, would know how far they are willing to go."

Mick asked "Do you know why, after all this time, they are still trying so hard to kill me?"

"You took down some key people and caused a great deal of humiliation. It's become the principle of the thing, much like the hunt for Osama bin Laden.”

Mick reached for her purse which was hanging behind the door and dug around inside and extracted a small automatic pistol. “Any more like this, or should I search you?” he asked.

Sasha held up her arms, coyly cocking her head, a sly smile on her lips, “You should search me. I advise you to be especially thorough.”

Chapter 9

Escape from the FBI

Basement of the Bellagio
2150 hours

There are no cameras in the ladies' room, one of the few areas in the entire complex not constantly watched from above, so the FBI was not aware that he had captured Sasha. Mick decided to get her away from the Bellagio, to allow more time to determine if she was what she claimed to be, before turning her over to either the FBI or the CIA. It was obvious that she had no part in the shootings, so she had committed no crime except taking some cash and cars from her temporary male companions. After chasing the other women out of the restroom, Mick used Sasha's small automatic to shoot the lock off the service door at the back wall. The service areas were likely being monitored, but he and Sasha might be able to get out on the street before Security or the FBI got organized.

Mick and Sasha walked silently down the maze of hallways beneath the massive hotel and casino. He was careful to keep Sasha in front of him, because she was not only well-trained but as yet could not be trusted. They passed the vault and money counting area which had been locked tight since the commotion above started. There were many personnel in the halls, most were in a state of near panic since the invasion of FBI agents and the subsequent gunfire.

"You have a car?" Mick asked.

"A borrowed one. They will be watching it."

Mick stopped, pausing to think, and then after noticing an Exit sign, made a sudden turn toward it. Pushing the door open, they entered the desert oven of hot night air. As it closed behind them, the sounds of the city returned. The Interstate highway was just behind the casino, the irregular hum of traffic hanging in the air. He firmly held Sasha's arm to make sure she understood not to run, and they started moving away from the casino, toward the parking deck on their left.

The stairs to the tram were just ahead, and after pausing to cautiously look around, they proceeded up the stairs. A large sign advertised that a tram came every twenty minutes, and the last stop was the Monte Carlo. That distance would give Mick long enough with her to have a conversation. The tram was the last place anyone would be looking, and they would be safe while they stayed out view of the many security cameras. Just after boarding the nearly empty automated tram, Mick's phone rang.

"Yes?"

"Mick, this is April. Do you have Sasha, and where are you?"

"I have her, and we are safe for the moment. I want

to talk with her first, and I'll get back to you when I decide what to do."

"Well, sure, have your conversation, but let us protect you and also keep her from getting away. Where are you?" she said more demandingly. Mick chose not to answer her and put the phone back in his pocket. Sasha sat silently watching him.

"Okay, Sasha. Let me have the whole story. If you don't convince me, I'm turning you over to the CIA. They are anxious to talk to you. The FBI will lock you up if they get you, but I'm willing to sit here and listen and not threaten you or use any force." She reached out and entwined her hand into his. He was reminded once again how powerful are a woman's natural tools. She looked sweetly and innocently at him, and her thin arms and soft skin hid well her predatory side. It is easy for a man to be taken in by a seductive woman, and nature has had a million years to perfect both feminine charm and the masculine response to it.

"Mick, have you ever shot a woman?" she asked softly.

"I have no rule against it and would have no hesitation to do it, but no, I have never shot a woman or even struck one."

Sasha snuggled a bit into his hard shoulder and held his arm with both of hers. "I feel safe for the first time in days," she said, rubbing her face against his sleeve.

"Don't bother using your sex appeal on me, Sasha. Talk," Mick said hoarsely.

Sasha took a deep breath and looked up at him

with sincerity. "I grew up in Vladivostok. My father was in the Russian Navy and became a heavy drinker. He was killed in a tavern brawl when I was ten. We moved back to Moscow, and I eventually went to Lomonosov to study English. I wanted to be a translator and travel. Before my education was complete, I was recruited by the Russian Security Service, what you call the GRU. You know, of course, that the SRU is still the KGB. We are not KGB. I was happy there, and they trained me in all sorts of things, including combat and foreign languages. When the time came for missions outside of Russia, they chose me because of my beauty, not because of any special ability. My first experience was in Germany, and I loved it there. That's where I first heard of Mick Grundy and what you did there. I didn't know whether to admire your courage or to hate you for your ruthless killing of our agents."

"Sasha, that is all old and useless information. What is the reason you are running and they are pursuing? We have little time here."

Sasha looked up, wrinkled her nose and squinted at him like a displeased child. "The head of the GRU unit responsible for covert operations is Anatoly Baranov. He is aggressively seeking to undermine all the Western governments, creating chaos and collapse, if possible. The pieces will be reassembled in the old Communist mold. Their agents will blame the capitalists and anyone with any money for causing despair and poverty of the people, and they will promote the loud voices of those who claim to represent the 'masses'. This is a tried and tested formula for takeover or neutralization of a country. America is a main target, and they have already started. They are using many ordinary people who don't realize what the end game really is, and they have active assistance from your naive leftist press. They are all pawns just like in the old days, and they will be used and discarded just like before. Alexander Sinitsin, who is also highly placed, has a different view. He and his followers feel that chaos and instability abroad will not help Russia and may pose a grave risk. Once started, you can never tell how a revolution will turn out and who will come to the top. It could result in the same thing as happened in Germany, leading to Hitler coming to power, or in our country, Stalin. We all could end up a lot worse that we are now. Word of Sinitsin's activity got out, and some of his people, including me, have had to flee for our lives. They can't touch Sinitsin himself yet because of his powerful friends. We need someone from outside to help us eliminate Baranov. He is in line for the presidency, and he is a danger to Russia as well as the rest of the world. Your intelligence services will never condone assassination of such a powerful man because of consequences, especially if the mission doesn't succeed. They will look the other way, though, if it is conducted from inside, by other Russians. That is why we sought you out. You have connections but are not connected. You have experience, and you are ruthless. Baranov knows about you, and he is the one trying so hard to get you. It isn't just for your past actions but for what you could do if you were recruited. His people discovered that we were trying to find you so they watched and let me do it, now they intend to kill us both."

"If you want me to kill this Baranov for you, you can forget it. I have no reason to trust you, and I don't know if anyone outside Russia can pick a good GRU man from a bad one. To us, they are the same. Russia has to solve its own problems. Asking a single man, or putting your hopes on one, is silly. Why should I risk my life to help solve your dilemma of who is in power?"

"Mick, they would stop hunting you. You would be an ally and friend instead of a perpetual enemy. Even if you don't help us, Baranov's people will eventually get you. Don't you see that you have nothing to lose and everything to gain?" Sasha spoke with so much passion that she attracted attention from the other passengers on the tram.

The tram reached its destination at the Monte Carlo, and the doors slammed open. He led her off, onto the platform, and they walked to the corner overlooking the perpetually busy Las Vegas Boulevard. They stood together, arms braced on the railing, watching the human parade go by. Even this far away, faint electronic rhythmic sounds of the slots could still be heard. Mick could feel Sasha's eyes studying his face, trying to determine any indication of his intentions. She moved closer to him and pressed against his arm, her perfume drifting into his consciousness, pulling on him with magnetic force. The multicolored glow of Las Vegas reflected from her skin and eyes in a dazzling display of beauty. Sasha was not the perfect, unblemished and idealized beauty that was April. Sasha was full-lipped, provocative, mysterious and hypnotically gorgeous in the way that allows some women simply to compel arousal in a man. He forced himself to look away from her, but she sensed his reaction and drew herself even closer to him.

Mick thought over what she had told him. It was tempting to get involved, but outrageously dangerous. He still had April's words of caution ringing in his ears. "You simply cannot trust her," she would have said. Lost in thought, he almost missed it, then snapped alert as he realized that two men had stopped below them and were looking up the stairs. One of them was holding a device and kept looking back at it. They were tracking something, probably Sasha, and had found her.

Mick pulled her away from the edge so that they couldn't be seen. "They have followed you and are right below us." Sasha recoiled in fear and put her hand to her mouth in surprise. Mick could feel her starting to tremble. He pulled her purse from her arm and flung it into a trash can. Behind him, he could hear the next tram approaching. "Give me your watch and jewelry, Sasha." She quickly complied and the items and her shoes were discarded into the trash. Mick quickly felt under her breasts for any devices but found nothing in her scant clothing. He pulled her into the tram car after the door opened, and they crouched down under the window. Mick caught a glimpse of the head of one of the men as he came up the staircase. The car was empty except for

Mick and Sasha, but the door remained open, patiently waiting for any other passengers who wanted to go back along the strip to the next casino. Just as the door finally started to close, a man's hand came into the opening, causing the door to reopen, and setting off an irritating chime. Mick stood up, drawing the small automatic pistol he had taken from Sasha. He was visible to the second man through the tram window but not by the one attempting to enter the cabin. Mick grabbed the man's arm and pulled him into the cabin forcefully enough that he fell into the closed door on the opposite side. A gunshot rang out, and glass near Mick shattered, as a bullet just missed his head. Mick pivoted into the door opening and fired three quick shots at the second man, dropping him to the floor. Another gunshot went off behind him, and he twisted around in time to see the first man falling. Sasha was standing with her feet apart, holding a large smoking handgun, and instantly firing a second shot into the man on the floor. Mick reached out and carefully took the gun from her hand.

"Where did this weapon come from?" he asked.

"I took it out of his holster as he fell. It was him or us. I had no choice."

"You have had good training, Sasha. You act quickly and reflexively, just as I do, and you probably saved my life just then." As he spoke, the tram door finally closed and the little train lurched forward. As they pulled away from the station, Mick could see several people discovering the body left on the platform. He searched the man on the floor and, as expected, found a fake FBI identification. After extracting the man's wallet, he took out the cash and threw the wallet back on the floor. "Expenses," he explained to the dead man. The bright sign for the Crystals stop came into view. He carefully wiped both guns down and dropped them beside the body. "We are getting off here," he said, this time gently taking her wrist.

"Why do you want to get rid of the guns, Mick? Don't you think that we might need them?" Sasha asked.

"I always discard guns after a shooting. You don't want to be caught with a gun used in a killing. Too many complications. I'll get another one soon," he explained. The door snapped open, and they walked away toward the open door of The Crystals Casino with composure, as if nothing extraordinary had happened. Sasha was barefooted, but no one seemed to notice. He led her toward the upscale shopping area, and they passed the most famous names in European clothing. Mick seemed to know what he wanted, and they entered the Pucci shop first. "Don't you think you should change your clothes?" he asked.

The clerk who came up to them looked both of them up and down in thinly veiled contempt. "Can I be of service, madam?" she said in Italian-accented English and turned her back to Mick.

Mick tapped the lady on the shoulder to get her attention, *"Voglio la signora vestita di buon gusto. Ha bisogno di quasi tutto e il costo non è un problema. Si prega di fare in modo e renderla felice."* ["I want the lady dressed in good taste. She needs almost everything and cost is not a problem. Please see to it and make her happy."]

The clerk's eyes opened widely, and she gave a little curtsey. *"Naturalmente, signore, io darle tutta la mia attenzione. Grazie per aver portato lei a noi"* ["Of course, sir, I will give her my full attention. Thank you for bringing her to us."]

Mick pulled out a credit card with an alias supplied by the CIA and gave it to the clerk. He could tell that Sasha clearly understood what had been said, but she remained passive, her face giving nothing away. He backed away to sit and observe as Sasha and the clerk moved around picking up items. When she disappeared into a changing booth, Mick picked up his phone. "I want to talk to Zeskie," he said into the phone without dialing. Within five seconds, the phone vibrated.

"Zeskie," a metallic voice said.

"Have your people been listening in during this whole thing?" Mick asked.

"Of course we listen, you know that," Zeskie answered in a soothing voice. "If you are asking me what I think, then I'll tell you that it seems to us that Sasha is legit. If she were part of a conspiracy to kill you, she would have done it instead of shoot her own fellow agent. On the other hand, it doesn't prove her story of good GRU people versus bad GRU people. She might actually believe the story, but that doesn't make it fact. The Russian Intelligence chiefs don't even trust their own agents with the truth."

"What do you suggest, Zeskie?"

"You are doing fine, Mick. Just go with it and see what happens. By the way, I'm delivering a package to you when you leave Pucci's, instead of tomorrow."

"You have to talk to April Chauncy, Zeskie. Explain to her that I have to believe this girl for now and travel East with her. April won't like it, and I don't know how to part from her without your help. Tell her that I'll be in touch, and I have come to greatly respect her."

"Sounds like something beyond a professional relationship. She would rather hear it from you, but I'll do what I can," Zeskie said.

Sasha came out of the dressing room in an attractive but simple shift made of a dark red shiny material with touches of silver at the arm opening and hem. She was still barefooted, moving like a ballerina, and she was careful to catch his eye so she could be sure he noticed. It was hard to remember that she had just shot one of her countrymen twice at close range when she had such elegantly graceful and feminine movements.

Mick's phone rang softly, and he reluctantly picked it up. "Remember me, Mick?" April asked. "You know, the partner you left behind looking frantically for you?"

"I'm sorry, April. There is a direction to things sometimes, and we are dragged along for the ride. Did Zeskie call you and explain?"

"Yeah, Zeskie called. There is really no excuse, Mick. My feelings are hurt, and I feel that you have reverted to the independent creature you always were. I guess that you don't need my help any longer.

And I hear that Sasha convinced you, so you are going to do her bidding, just like all the other males she picked up and later discarded."

"I was asked to see this through, April, and I'm just doing my job. I want to tell you how very much I enjoy working with you and how much respect I have for you, and I hope we can still be partners and friends when this thing is over."

April raised her voice, and Mick was tempted to hold the phone away from his ear. "It's obvious that you don't value my opinion, because you are putting yourself in the jaws of the enemy. I'll tell you again, and I hope it rings in your ears. YOU CAN'T TRUST SASHA OR BELIEVE WHAT SHE TELLS YOU! Did you hear that?"

"Thanks, April. I mean it. Thanks. Got to go, but I'll see you as soon as I can." Mick put away the phone and continued to watch the visually magnetic Sasha fluidly move around the shop.

Chapter 10

Traveling Companion

McCarran International Airport, Las Vegas
0515 hours

They sat shoulder to shoulder in the terminal waiting for the plane to Germany, boarding in 15 minutes. As Zeskie promised, a courier had handed Mick an unmarked brown paper package as they left the clothing store. Mick nodded to him and tucked it under his arm. "One more stop," Mick explained, and they headed to Gucci, just down the hall. Mick found what he was looking for quickly, selecting a well-tailored leather jacket nearly identical to the one he was given by his father-in-law just before his wedding to Anna. The one he left behind when he had to leave Germany. When he put it on, he felt a strange feeling of *deja vu* come over him, but one with the wrong woman nearby. He knew that it could never be the same, the happiness he had felt then, the love he would never feel again.

He excused himself to visit the restroom and opened the package supplied by Zeskie. There was another unmarked 45 caliber automatic handgun and passports in yet another alias for each of them.

Zeskie had also supplied papers identifying him as a U.S. Marshal and authorizing him to carry a weapon on any flight. Two plane tickets to Berlin, for a flight due to leave at 0600, were tucked in an envelop bulging with Euros.

"Passenger Wells, please report to the boarding area of United Flight 414," came over the loudspeaker. It took Mick a second to remember that he was Frank Wells. He touched Sasha on the shoulder and said, "That's us. Let's go," and they got up together. Neither had any luggage but the boarding personnel weren't surprised since passenger Wells had been pointed out as part of the security team.

"Where would you like to be seated, sir?" the attendant asked conspiratorially.

"It's better if I ride in the last seat on the aisle side, and I prefer to have my right arm on the outside. That way I can easily watch the passengers. This lady will sit beside me," Mick informed her.

They boarded first, and Mick watched the other passengers carefully as the plane slowly filled. There were no obvious threats, and he began to relax a bit as the plane accelerated into the morning sky.

"Your people are very efficient, Mick," Sasha said into his ear. "To get this in motion only minutes after you found me...well, our side couldn't have done it. They must have expected you to be successful all along," she remarked, accompanied by a sidelong glance. He nodded but didn't respond. Mick knew that Zeskie would be there in Germany after they arrived and that Sasha was about to be subjected to intensive grilling prior to any agreement from the CIA to proceed with her scheme. There was a need to keep this very secret, in case there was an assassination of one faction of the GRU by another. The CIA could not afford to be seen to have any role or take sides in a Russian internal struggle.

Sasha snuggled up to him, wrapping around his arm. Her hair was just under his nose, and her perfume wafted up to him. He looked her over as he thought about their relationship. She had saved his life on the Tram, but he still had reservations about her motives. There was no doubt about her utter sex appeal, though. This was one woman that he would like to see without clothing. Her loose clothing exposed enough cleavage of her breasts to arouse him when he looked for too long, and he tried unsuccessfully to put her body out of his thoughts. Impossible. He knew that he could resist giving in to a sexual encounter because that would complicate things too much, but the magnetic pull of her sexuality was strong. He let out a big sigh, and she glanced up at his face and gave him a knowing look. Things were going just as she wanted.

Chapter 10

Chapter 11

Interviewing Spies

F BI Headquarters, Las Vegas
0900 hours

April Chauncy closed the meeting room door and sat down. Gathered around the table were six of the agents involved in the previous day's activities. Most had a Styrofoam cup of coffee at hand and a variety of paper pads or electronic devices lying on the polished wood top.

"Tom. Report please," she asked.

Agent Tom Cavendaw cleared his throat and glanced around. He flipped through his yellow ledger finding the summary page. "There were eight fatalities by gunshot, all apparently Russian, but we are still checking. Four of them had forged ID representing them as FBI. Very well done, I might add. We had to check the numbers and photos with Washington to be sure. The others had no identity at all on them. We collected DNA, prints and photos, and they are being processed in Washington and at Langley. One of the guns, that is, the gun collected by Special Agent Chauncy, was used in two previous fatal shootings in Tacoma. We have two suspects in custody who were rounded up in the sweep in the Bellagio casino area. So far, we can't get them to even say a word, and they carried no identification." He looked up to be sure that he had been understood.

One of the agents put his hand up and started speaking. "All present know that these two are Russian. You can even smell it on them. I say that we turn them over to the CIA who will export them to Cuba for some really intensive questioning."

"At least threaten them with it," someone suggested.

Special Agent Chauncy put up her hand to silence the room. "No, guys, we aren't turning them over to anyone. Since they are classified as terrorists, we can hold them indefinitely. I would like to see an effort made to turn them to our side. We have all the cards. Their side cannot admit that they are Russians without an explanation as to what they were up to. The Director is furious about the use of fake FBI credentials, and he is calling this an act of war on the part of the Russians. Mother Russia is bound to deny any connection with our captured spies, so we can take our time."

Another hand went up. "Can you give us more information about this Mick Grundy? Like, who is he and where did he go? Was he the one who killed eight men?"

"Seven. He killed seven. We think that Sasha killed one of them. That was the one left in the Tram car. Who is he? Some of that is classified above our level, but to summarize, I can tell you the short story. He was trained by Army Special Forces, stationed in Germany and went on several covert missions jointly with the CIA. He was severely wounded at least twice and was discharged from the Army. He is a pet of the CIA and has high connections. What they do with him is anyone's guess. He is a natural killer and never hesitates to use force. His wife was killed by Russians on the first day of his honeymoon; they pursue him still. He is highly skilled with weapons or deception and fluent in several languages. I consider him to be the most dangerous man I have ever encountered, and I am thankful that he is on our side. The Russians currently are trying to recruit him to assist in some way with an assassination of a high official in the Russian Intelligence Service. It is very possible that they just want to capture and kill him instead. I know that he left for Germany with Sasha this morning, but I don't know any more than that." Special Agent Chauncy paused and looked off at the wall lost in thought.

"What's next, Special Agent? Got any assignments for us?" one of them asked.

She came back to focus and looked over the group. "The action has moved on. I'm sure everyone from the other side has left. What remains for us is good old-fashioned police work. We have to find out everything we can about the spies and assassins who were here. Where did they come from, and who directed them. We have to process the hard evidence we have and try to get some cooperation from the two who were captured. I will admit that it is unlikely that they will cooperate or even know anything useful, but it's what we have."

"What about all the complaints from the casinos about the disruption?" Tom asked softly.

"They can take their complaints and stick them up their ample asses, or they can write the local congressmen and see where it gets them. Someone find me a good Russian translator. I want to visit our captives before I go to Washington later today. I'll have a list of assignments posted before I leave."

April Chauncy rounded the corner just ahead of her two accompanying males. One was an FBI agent proficient in Russian, and the other was a young agent selected by April because of his muscularity and his hard-looking face. She approached the first room and studied the monitor outside the room before entering. The two male agents were right behind her when she entered the small cell. Their prisoner was sitting on the cot, still fully dressed in his cheap black suit. He looked up with disinterest at the new arrivals but did a second look when he saw Special Agent Chauncy. He looked her up and down slowly as if appraising her for a possible sexual encounter and smiled suggestively and knowingly. The man reeked of body odors, needed a shave, and appeared to be in his late thirties with unruly dark hair and exuberant eyebrows.

"I am Special Agent Chauncy. We are here to try to get cooperation from you before we resort to other methods." She studied his face for any sign that he understood. Seeing none, she motioned for the translator who repeated her words in Russian. Still no indication or even flicker from him that he took it in. She continued, "Eight of your fellow agents were slain in this little endeavor, and what do we find on the bodies? Our own FBI badges and ID. We are more than a little unhappy. You, on the other hand, had no ID of any kind. You have no nationality as far as we are concerned, so we can cut you into little pieces if we want, with no one complaining." She did not signal for translation and none was given. She looked over her shoulder at Michael, who stepped forward and grabbed the prisoner by the clothing and lifted him into the air. As he dangled, Michael hit him hard in the abdomen and threw him to the floor gasping for air. "As you can see," April continued, "we are not going to play nice. Either you start talking or I'm walking out of the room and leaving you with Michael." The man on the floor was heaving and drooling, but his eyes narrowed and didn't leave her face, projecting his antagonism and defiance. She shrugged, "Do what it takes, and I'll be back to see if he can be encouraged to do this the easy way." She turned and headed toward the door when the man made a sound. April stopped and turned half back toward him.

"Wait! I need a deal." He croaked out in accented English.

"No deals," she said and left the room. She and the translator could hear the sounds of flesh being struck, followed by groans. They proceeded to the next room which was down the hall a short distance. Again, she studied the man on the room monitor before entering. They swept into the room and stood in front of him as he lounged comfortably on the cot. He had a smirk on his face as if to tell them that they could expect nothing from him.

April smiled back at him and said, "Your fellow down the hall is talking, and all we had to do is beat him a little. You have no value to us at all, and the CIA is coming to pick you up. I sure hope you show your little smile to them, because they enjoy showing you the dark side of captivity. By the way, since you claim no country of origin and none claims you, you will be deposited in the ocean somewhere between our coast and Cuba when they are done. There is a shark out there with your name on its lips waiting for you to arrive." She gave a little laugh and reached for the door.

"Wait! Perhaps I can be useful to you," the man said.

April looked back at him and answered, "You are as useful as a turd floating in the toilet," then she laughed and went back into the hall. As the door closed behind them, they could see the man folded up on the bed rocking back and forth as if in agony, his head buried into his knees. April turned to the agent translator and said, "I have to get to the airport to catch a flight. I want Michael to come in and work him over when he is done with the first one. Let them both stew overnight, and then start the interview process. I want to know every detail of their crummy lives, but most of all, I want to know about this operation, who their superiors are, where they are and what the orders were. When you are done, turn them over to the CIA."

The agent answered, "Yes, ma'am. Are you coming back from Washington?"

"Unknown. I also do what they tell me. Until I am reassigned, this team is under my direction, and all my orders are to be carried out. I will be in contact, and we will go from there." She checked her watch, then nodded goodbye and walked briskly down the long hall.

Chapter 12

Meeting the Boss

J. Edgar Hoover Building, Washington
0845 hours

April pushed the large glass door open, entering the lobby of FBI Headquarters. She had been instructed to display her badge outside her clothing when in this building, and she felt again to see if it was in place. It was just where she put it on the left jacket pocket of her regulation blue suit. She had her hair up and had been especially sparse with her makeup this morning. After arriving from Las Vegas, she only had time for a brief nap and, as yet, no breakfast or coffee. There is always tension when meeting a superior, and you always have to be ready for insults and criticism. Usually, she was very good at it, and her beauty inhibited most males from being harsh to her. She stopped at the desk and handed over her badge. The officer on duty looked at it carefully and then back at her several times before returning it to her.

"Special Agent Chauncy, you are to accompany Agent Towles, who is behind you," he said. She turned to see that Agent Towles was indeed standing right behind her. Agent Towles was wearing a mannequin face and was going to go strictly by protocol.

"Come this way, Special Agent," he beckoned, without a flicker of warmth or welcome, turning his back and moving away. They went in single file to a small room off the main corridor. "New procedure, Special Agent Chauncy. You are to surrender all weapons at this time. They will be returned to you as you exit the building." He opened a large envelope lying on the desk with her name already affixed to the front.

April pulled her service pistol and placed it on the desk. "If you try to pat me down, I'll split your lip for you," she said evenly.

"Not to worry, Special Agent. But if the alarm on the metal detector goes off, then we will get our chance to tussle," he replied, just as evenly.

She passed through the machine without its making a sound and was led to the elevators. "You are to go to the Director's office on the top floor where they are expecting you. Good luck, Special Agent." He gave her a factory smile before leaving her alone, waiting for the special elevator to the top.

After arriving at the designated stop, the elevator door snapped open to reveal a tall, handsome, young black man standing in front of the elevators. He had an inviting smile and extended his hand for a handshake. "Welcome, Special Agent Chauncy! I am Agent Sam Watson, and I will be your assistant for this meeting. Please follow me." He led her into another small room off the main corridor. On the table in the center of the room was a large stack of folders. He motioned for her to pull up a chair. "We need to get you up to speed before the meeting starts. They hate hesitation and indecision, and everyone is always on a tight schedule, so we aim for efficiency." He smiled again at her and appeared to be waiting for her response.

"I thought I was here to meet with the Director. I am confused about what is happening. Who are the 'they' that you mentioned?" she asked.

Agent Watson rolled his eyes. "They are somewhat ill-defined. It depends on who shows up or who is designated to replace them. To be sure, this is a high level meeting, and we will have representatives from G-2, CIA, NSB and State. I believe you have met Major General Chuck Adams from G-2 previously. Your job is to report when asked about your present mission. Don't give opinions unless asked. Do not ask questions unless invited to do so. Remain standing after your report unless asked to sit down. Exit promptly when dismissed. Got that?"

"No," she said. "Why am I here? I could have just filed a report and a scant one at that. I don't have much information to give them." She looked worried, and her smooth brow furrowed.

"I can't tell you why you are here, Special Agent," he answered. "Someone at a high level requested it. I would venture that you will be asked to join a new group or mission, but we will have to wait and see. Meanwhile, I want you to go over the stack of documents here, and I'll go and get you a cup of your favorite beverage while the meeting assembles and you are asked to go in."

She pursed her lips and said, "Cappuccino, sprinkle of powdered sugar?"

"Right away!" he said and left the room.

She reached for the stack of documents and could see various seals representing some of the many intelligence agencies of the U.S. Government. She selected the one from the CIA and slid out the contents. One stack was the printed copy of most of the conversations between her and Mick Grundy. She was stunned at the detail. As she flipped through, she realized that everything she had ever uttered was there in print. If they had had physical contact, the grunts would be there also. There were photos included of her and Mick in various locations. There were more of Sasha, largely taken from surveillance cameras in the Las Vegas casinos. Also photos of the slain Russian agents and of the driver killed in Tacoma including one of the lawyer sprawled across his living room floor. She put the papers back in the envelope and reached for another one, when the door opened.

"Here you are, Special Agent," he said and handed her a Styrofoam cup of black coffee. "Couldn't locate any powdered sugar. Sorry," he said with his now irritating smile. You have about ten minutes, and I will be back for you when they are ready." He smiled again and left the room. She reached for the envelope from the State Department. It was a thorough analysis of the Russian GRU and focused on two individuals, Anatoly Baranov and Alexander Sinitsin. Several photographs were included of the men in various activities. She flipped to the summary and quickly read it. It outlined rumors of a conflict between the men in their reach for higher position within the Russian administration. Sinitsin was related to President Putin somewhat distantly but enough to insulate him. Baranov was former Soviet Army and had a long list of previous friendships which included still active high ranking officers They both wanted to rise to become director of the GRU replacing the fossilized present leadership. The analyst who authored the document felt that both were a risk to the U.S. in different ways and either would invigorate the GRU and ultimately cause problems for the U.S. There was no course of action recommended. The first page was initialed by the Secretary of State indicating that she had read it. She put the papers away and reached for another envelope, when the door opened.

"Ready?" Agent Watson asked with his little smile.

April thought, hell, no! I would rather have a knife fight than go in there, but she didn't say it. She was led down a broad carpeted corridor toward a large, carved, double, wooden door. There were two heavily-built men standing on each side and a female clerk seated at a small folding table.

The clerk smiled up at her and said, "Good morning, Special Agent. May I have your badge please?" April handed it over and watched as the woman scanned it into the small machine on the table. After a moment, she handed it back with another smile. The door opened to show a small gathering around a large dark wood table. The outside walls were adorned with huge LED screens which were displaying a variety of images. Assistants scurried around the outside of the table behind the seated guests. Someone made a motion for April to come forward, and she walked to the head of the table and stood behind a chair. General Adams rose from his chair and walked up to her with his hand extended.

"Good morning, Special Agent Chauncy, good morning. It's so nice to see you again, and welcome to our meeting," he said with sincerity while shaking her hand. April glanced at the other members of the group and could see some disgruntled faces at this display of courtesy by the General. General Adams pulled the chair our for her and said, "Please, seat yourself, and if you need any beverage or water, we will see that you get it."

"Thank you, sir," April said, sitting down and looking at the name plates in front of the five others at the table. The closest was "Manson Carver, Assistant Secretary of State." Mr. Carver was busy with his paperwork and didn't look up at her. Across from him was "Karen Kindle, Acting Director, Central Intelligence Agency." Director Kindle was looking her way and didn't acknowledge April's nod of greeting. Down from her was the General's plate which read "Major General Charles Adams, United States Army." Across from the General, the plate read "Mary Jussup Carver Stanley, Federal Bureau of Investigation, Directorate of Intelligence." Director Stanley had a larger plate than the others which was fitting in that she was an exceptionally large person.

She was looking disapprovingly at April and didn't return April's try at acknowledgment. Each official had a stack of paperwork and a laptop as well as a personal assistant standing somewhere behind.

As General Adams returned to his place, he remained standing and looked at the others briefly before talking. "You all have been updated about the current status of the Russian agent called Sasha. Special Agent Chauncy has been at the heart of the investigation so far, and she has been invited here to give us a live interpretation of all the paperwork in front of us about this issue." He paused, looking for any interruption, and saw that he had everyone's attention.

"I have a question," Director Stanley said loudly. Everyone looked toward her. "I want to know from you, General, and from you, Director Kindle, why the primary agent working on this case is not an active agent and has a horrible record of crimes against humanity, and especially against our friends in the Democratic Russian Republic?" She glowered, waiting for the confrontation which was sure to follow such a remark. She looked like a large angry toad perched on top of a rock daring an attack by enemies.

"If you read your briefing papers, you would know that the Russians themselves selected Mick Grundy, and their countrymen have left a trail of dead bodies across two states, most of them their own," General Adams said with a rising voice. "Furthermore, our allies, the Russians, have been impersonating FBI agents in their quest to kill Grundy. I should think that you should direct your irritation toward them and not at one of our nation's finest men."

"I would like to add to that comment, General," said Director Kindle. She rose to her feet and looked at Director Stanley. "Mary, you and I are both political appointees. Neither one of us had a background in intelligence matters, and both of us will disappear and be forgotten at the whim of whoever occupies the White House. I plan to listen and learn from the real spooks, and I would advise you to do the same. I got the same rush from the Russian diplomats and phone calls of well wishing from the GRU people in Moscow. I felt like I was back in high school being courted for the prom. Don't get taken in by them. I looked over Grundy's record, and I am impressed by the man. We are lucky to have him working the case, thanks to the General here. My impression remains that there are a lot of good people in Russia, but none are in the present government." She sat back down to the hateful stare of Director Stanley across from her.

The man from State, Mr. Carver, spoke up at last. "We have no time to waste this morning on politics. I don't have a clear idea of our role in this mission or even the goals of it. It appears that the Russians are directing this, or pulling the strings, and things are going just as somebody wanted. But, where are we going and what happens when we get there?" He was looking at General Adams for answers and avoided looking at April.

General Adams chuckled. "Well, that is why we are here, isn't it?" He pulled his chair out and sat down.

"April, can you tell us about this case, from your point of view, up to the moment?" he asked.

April swallowed hard and looked around. "Thank you all for allowing me to attend this conference. As you know, we were pursuing a young Russian woman who was involved in two shootings in Tacoma. She identified herself to Mr. Grundy as a Russian Intelligence officer and described a possible conflict in the Russian GRU. She said that one side wanted help from Grundy. The other side apparently had different ideas, and two men were killed. They, and we, pursued her to Las Vegas where eight Russians were shot while attempting to kill Mick Grundy. One of them was killed by this woman calling herself Sasha. Since that time, she and Grundy traveled to Berlin with American assistance, and I have not been informed since they arrived of what else has happened. We also captured two men, who were without identity, and whom we assume are Russian agents, and they are being interrogated at this moment in Las Vegas and will be turned over to another agency when we are done." As she finished, one of the large screens filled with the image of Ron Zeskie and sitting beside him was the man of interest himself, Mick Grundy. It was obvious that there was a video link and each party could see the other. Mick gave a little wave which April felt was for her.

General Adams said, "Thank you, Special Agent Chauncy, for your summary." He turned toward Zeskie and Grundy and said, "Welcome to our conference, gentlemen. Do you have an update for us on that end?"

Zeskie cleared his throat, "General, good to see you again. And you also, Acting Director Kindle. We have Sasha in our custody, and she is undergoing the process of interview at this time. She is being cooperative, but this sort of thing takes several days to be as rigorous as we must be for a complicated matter. We need to be sure that what she says, she believes. The truth is a different matter, but there we have some help. We have two recent defectors from the GRU, one of whom was recently wounded in a gunfight among Russians. He has decided to seek asylum with us and is talking his head off. He does confirm that there is an ideologic struggle going on right now. After talking to him extensively, I feel that although both sides are nationalistic Russians, one of the sides would appear to prefer a more democratic Russia. We always wanted a democratic Russia, even though it might pursue a course contrary to our needs. The bad can rise to the top in a democracy, as we know from our own experience, but it is better than a return to Stalinism."

Director Stanley grunted with the effort to raise her ponderous mass to her feet and shouted, "How dare you demean this administration with the snide comment about the bad rising to the top in this country. How dare you say such a thing in front of these loyal Americans, while you are safe in Germany hiding who knows where and doing who knows what against innocent people abroad in the name of the American people." She wiped the drool from her lip and glared defiantly around the room, searching for someone who would dare to have another opinion to voice. The man from State had his head down and diligently shuffled his papers. General Adams sighed and tossed his pen on the table.

Director Kindle also got up and glared across the table at this huge angry woman from the FBI. Karen Kindle stood five feet two and weighed only just over one hundred pounds, but she was not about to let one of her agents take any verbal abuse from this hack political appointee across from her. "Director Stanley. I did not hear Agent Zeskie say anything at all about the present administration. In fact, this administration is always stating in so many words that the previous administration was incompetent and the cause all of our present problems. You are in error to insult my agent in this manner. I resent it for him and also personally, and I resent it for the American people whom you want to protect from something. Either tone your rhetoric down, or I will cancel this meeting, and the CIA will proceed with this operation without you being informed anything about it. You are here as a courtesy in order to fulfill the desire for our intelligence operatives to work together to avoid duplication and to share information. You are not here to criticize anything or anyone. Save it for a stump speech, but shut up in here. Am I clear or not, Director Stanley?"

Director Stanley slowly and petulantly sat down and then so did Director Kindle. General Adams turned toward the monitor and said, "Mr. Grundy, do you have anything to add?"

Mick smiled and said, "Hi, General. Good to see you again. I think we have to wait for Ron's people to have a chance at her. I believe her story, though I should qualify that to mean that I believe that she is stating what she was told. We are still not clear about what she wants, but she is only a messenger and bait to get me to talk to a more highly placed individual who reportedly has a plan. What you people should do is to figure out how you want this thing to come out in the end. From here, I can't tell the bad guys from the good, because they all lie as far as I am concerned. Previously, Sasha told me that Alexander Sinitsin's people are the ones who want to recruit me, but so far, I haven't been told the reason."

Zeskie spoke up. "That is about what we hear. Alexander Sinitsin is supposed to be the one wanting a true democracy in Russia. Remember where we heard that before? It was Putin's words before he came to power."

General Adams stood and walked around the room while he spoke, "Here is the way I view this. We don't yet know if it is an opportunity for us to help bring positive change in Russia or to help yet another autocrat come to power. We are not sure that the goal on the other side is to trap and embarrass us for meddling in the internal affairs of a foreign government or simply to get their hands on Mick Grundy and have a show trial with him. I suggest that we continue to gather information for now and withhold any overt action, until we know what cards are being played. To that end, I would like Special Agent April Chauncy to be assigned to the FBI office in Berlin. There, she can work with Zeskie and

Grundy to form an action plan we can all be happy with." He stopped and looked at Director Stanley. Since she was the appointed head of the FBI's NSB unit, it was appropriate that she approve the transfer.

Director Stanley looked surprised when she realized that everyone was looking at her, waiting for a response. She stared at April, who was at the head of the table, before drawing herself up for an answer. "I could see the deference she was shown by you, General. Is her looks the reason for her preferred treatment, or is it your boy, Mick Grundy's, attraction for her the basis for your request? We all saw the little wave. There are hundreds of qualified FBI agents to choose from, some of them already in Berlin. Frankly, I was unimpressed with her report, and my instinct is to discharge her from any more duties associated with this matter."

This time the General was angry and quickly said, "My dear Director. First of all, I cleared this transfer this morning with your superior, the Director of the FBI. I was just giving you the chance to be a member of this group, a mistake I won't make again." He was about to go on and was interrupted by Director Karen Kindle.

"Forgive me, General Adams, for interrupting again, but I can't let this go uncontested." She looked at April and smiled briefly. "Marked beauty like Special Agent Chauncy has is an asset. It's true that beauty attracts attention, but it is also distracting and disarming and is as much a tool as a handgun. From her files, it is obvious that this young woman is aware of what it means to be beautiful and how to use it in her work. I hope that Mick Grundy is attracted to her, because I would think less of him if he wasn't. They have worked together well in the recent past, and I think Mr. Grundy and Mr. Zeskie would admit that few people have ever worked seamlessly with Mick previously. These three agents are well chosen to work together and to help us decide what is in the best interest of the United States of America."

For the first time Mr. Carver aroused himself and sat up straight. "I agree, General, that the team you have put together is a good one, and I look forward to them acquiring more information so that we can put this issue at rest. You have my full support."

Smiling, General Adams turned toward the screen with the image of Zeskie and Grundy and said, "There it is. You are charged with figuring this thing out. Please don't get killed in the process, Grundy, because we will have need of you again."

Mick Grundy leaned forward and said, "May I say something to Director Kindle?"

"Go ahead, I'm listening," she said

"Don't worry, I am," he said with a little wave and smile and then the screen went dark.

Chapter 13

April in Berlin

FBI Office, U.S. Embassy, Berlin Germany
1030 hours

April opened the door to the conference room and saw Mick and Zeskie were already there. They both got up smiling and came around the table to greet her.

"Good to see you again, Partner!" Mick said and hugged her. "Did you have a good trip?" he asked. Zeskie extended his hand for a shake, while she embraced Mick.

"Good to see you both also," April said. "Please sit back down and fill me in on all I've missed while traveling." She pulled up a chair, and Mick poured her a cup of coffee. "By the way, is she here?" April asked.

Zeskie answered, "They should be arriving shortly. You must remember that we have been at her for three days, and she was sleep deprived during the entire time as part of the interrogation. She is likely to be angry and also distracted, so it wouldn't be a good time to bear down on her very hard." He smiled at April to make his point.

"Sure, I understand," she said. "Get anything out of her useful to us?"

Mick spoke up, "It appears that everything she knows comes from her station chief, a chap code named Ivanoff." She hasn't actually met anyone higher in command. We are convinced that she truly believes that the other faction means to kill her for attempting to recruit me, but she is unwilling to act as a double agent for us. There are few options for her if we turn her loose, except to contact Ivanoff and seek his protection. She was given a method of contacting him, which she did not fully divulge, but to me smells like some kind of letter drop. Her associates in America were either left behind or gathered up by the other side. It comes down to her sticking her neck out when she tries to make contact. She might even be eliminated, because her contact has been compromised or even switched allegiance in her absence. She also might be suspected of cooperation with us and finished as a Russian operative. Most of the scenarios I can envision would go badly for her."

Zeskie added, "I agree with Mick. She may not turn out to be useful after all. What Mick didn't say is that if he sticks with her when she contacts her superiors, they might string her along just to get at him. This is a risky situation, and there are no easy answers."

April said, "The two we captured in Las Vegas were nearly saying the same thing. They were working under Anatoly Baranov's group and were instructed to kill Sasha, but only after she led them to Mick.

They both confirm a struggle for the leadership of the entire GRU, putting the winner in a position of probable advancement to the top levels of Russian government in the future. It is an important struggle, and the outcome will be felt by the world for a long time to come. Zeskie, does the CIA have any independent assessment of Anatoly Baranov or Alexander Sinitsin?"

"Well," then he paused briefly gathering his thoughts, "we can trace both of them in depth from birth to now, and we know where they are and what they are doing. We will never know what they are thinking or planning or what is in their hearts. Only history will record that after the fact."

Mick blurted, "I want to meet this Alexander Sinitsin myself and in person."

"Want to also walk on the surface of the moon barefooted, Mick?" Zeskie laughed.

They were interrupted by Zeskie's phone, and shortly afterward, April's phone rang. The package had arrived, and they were bringing her up right now. They opened the door and sat in silence, listening for the sounds of feet approaching, and they had a short wait. Mick went into the hall and saw Sasha between two large men, slowly being walked toward them. They both supported her arms, and she looked wobbly and unkempt. She was wearing the same dress that Mick had purchased for her in Vegas, and her long hair partly obscured her face. As they came by, Mick could see one eye looking at him through the hair. The group turned into the conference room, and they helped her to a chair. She slumped into it with her face covered by her long hair. Mick knelt in front of her and pushed away the hair.

"Hi. Sorry that you had to go through this. Hope it wasn't too rough. They tell me that you were cooperative, and they are finished with you. You awake enough to understand me?" She nodded yes, but didn't speak. "You met Mr. Zeskie when you came in. He is here with an agent from the U.S. who is standing behind you." Sasha turned slowly and glanced up at April. They stared at each other for a moment without comment. April moved around her until she was at the front of the chair.

"Sasha, I am FBI Special Agent Chauncy, and you are in the FBI offices at the American Embassy. We are authorized to hold you here until the charges filed against you in the U.S. can be addressed. These are numerous and include credit card fraud, grand theft auto, transporting stolen merchandise across state lines, and physical assault. I am willing to drop the charges in return for the cooperation you have shown so far. In view of your extensive interrogation and your present condition, you will be given secure quarters here to recover, and in a couple of days we will discuss what the future holds."

Sasha ignored her and leaned forward and wrapped her arms around Mick, who was still kneeling, and pulled toward him until they were in an embrace. Mick stood, picking Sasha up in his arms as he rose. "Let's put her to bed for a while and let her recover. Lead the way, please." As Sasha came by, April could see one of her eyes, and the message was clear. "I have him right where I want." The four of them slowly disappeared down the hall with Zeskie in tow. When they reached the room, Mick lowered her into the bed and covered her up with more tenderness than April wanted to see. The room was actually a suite with a small, well-stocked kitchen and a well-appointed bath. Mick turned off the lights, and they locked the door from the outside.

In the hall, Mick turned to Zeskie and said, "Any way we can contact this Alexander Sinitsin and arrange a meeting with him in exchange for his valuable agent, Sasha?

Zeskie thought about it and said, "Really, no. Not without going through channels which would tell his competition what they want to know. I think you are going to have to rely on Sasha's supervisor here in Berlin, when she is up for it. We owe it to her to go over the risks to her and to you if she attempts to make contact. It's the only way, however."

Mick looked disappointed but was unable to refute what Zeskie said. "Can you locate my brother for me? I think I have time to see him while Sasha recovers. Perhaps he can make a suggestion."

"I'll find him for you, but I don't want German Intelligence in on this case. The more who know adds exponential risks and increases the chance of failure. Take April with you, and she will keep you quiet." April was standing with them and nodded agreement. Zeskie added, "Why don't you two go out on the town on me tonight, and let me work on some things. I'll call you if I need you; otherwise, we will meet here tomorrow, and we'll talk with Sasha together. By the way, I'm turning off the listening device on your phone for just tonight. Your privacy is guaranteed. Enjoy." With the last comment and a pat on Mick's back, Zeskie strolled down the hall away from them.

Remyhouse Gypsy Restaurant
1900 hours

April smiled and raised her cocktail glass to Mick's with a 'clink'. "This place is a perfect choice, Mick," she said. "I am having such a good time, and it really is good to get away from our work and just let go." She looked around the large room and gave a big sigh. "I didn't know places like this still were around." The band was playing a big band number at the moment, and about half the diners were on the dance floor. April knew a scattering amount about the German language from one semester in college, but she was with a true master. She knew that he was showing off for her like a high school date, but it was a lot of fun to watch him strike up a conversation and converse fluently in almost any language. She began to realize what a chameleon he truly was. He could be threatening or soft as butter, and he was different to each person he met. The music started with an old and slow dance number, and Mick stood up and offered her his hand. When they reached the dance floor, he put his hand on her waist and pulled her toward him, and they danced. And how they danced.

"Where did you learn to dance like this, Mick?" she whispered into his ear.

"My adoptive parents were German, and they got me started early. Along with languages, they both were passionate about dancing. I took lessons for years, but thank you for the compliment. It is my pleasure to have you in my arms tonight. You are the very first woman to dance with me since high school." He spun her around and drew her back in.

Mick leaned back in his chair and took in the atmosphere. On the ceiling was a glittering glass globe with a thousand reflective faces sending a constantly changing shower of bright spots of different color across the room. The live band was playing hits from prewar America, and around the room there was laughter and the sounds of tinkling glass. Across from him was the incredibly beautiful April who smiled at him broadly each time he looked in her direction. The table was small enough that their conversation was low and private.

"What about you, April? You know my life inside and out. It's your turn to come clean about your past and your previous loves," Mick said with his rough whisper.

"I had a boring childhood and was raised in a Chicago suburb by my parents. My dad was a dentist, and my mom was a stay-at-home mother who doted on me. I had lessons in about every available subject but was master of none. I went to college in nearby Aurora, then to two years of law school in Chicago, before dropping out to join the FBI. Why they wanted me so badly is anyone's guess. It may have been just to fill the female quota at the time. Boyfriends? Yes, I had my share, but none got too close, and I never had any proposals. Usually, they are attracted by my appearance, and they forget that I also have a personality and free will. When they find that out, they are gone. The FBI has treated me well. I get to travel a lot and, at times, meet the most interesting people, such as you." She finished by looking steadily into his eyes until he blinked.

After a couple of hours on the dance floor and a good meal, Mick said, "Let's try something different." He threw some cash on the table, and they grabbed their coats. Out at the curb, April heard him tell the cabbie, *"Maria am Ostbahnhof."* The man nodded, and they piled in.

"What's up, Mick?" April asked. He just smiled at her as they drove into the darkness. The taxi pulled up at a venue with a long line waiting to be admitted. The pulsating sounds of Techno drifted into the street past the doormen. Most of the would-be patrons were young and dressed flamboyantly, but there were a few reaching toward middle age. Mick motioned to her to wait as he made his way past the crowd to the door. He huddled with one of the men for a moment, then seemed to push some cash into the man's hand. He twisted toward her and motioned for her to come up.

While they were heading into the dance area, April asked him, "How did you get in so fast?"

"I just asked him in my best Irish accent if he knew Tommy Robinson," he said smiling. April drew a blank but shrugged and held his arm. The large room was ablaze with moving lights and people, the music loud enough to feel in your chest. April felt too old for the crowd and too well-dressed, but they were out for a good time, and this was a different sort of dancing for sure. During a dance, one man tapped her on the shoulder and signaled her to come with him. She said "NO" as loudly as she could, but he grabbed her arm playfully, but forcefully, and was attempting to pull her away. She could sense that Mick was moving to intervene, but she acted on her own before he did. She twisted her arm to wrap the man's wrist in her grasp, jerking and rotating forcefully, bringing him to his knees in one swift motion. The man got up quickly but saw Mick standing in front of him. He backed away and left the floor.

"Time to go, April," Mick said in a brief lull in the music. She agreed, and they started out. As they approached the exit hall, they could see two men standing in the shadows near the door. One was much larger than the other, and as they grew closer, Mick could tell that the shorter one was the man whom April had humiliated earlier. Mick gently pushed April behind him and walked up slowly to stand in front of the men. He didn't say anything to them and waited for any response. The two men sensed that they had made a mistake and that the man in front of them would respond with deadly force if provoked. There was a moment of silence while slow positioning movements by Mick showed that he was ready to strike out at any time. The larger man would be first, and he realized that he was no match for this stranger.

"So, you say that you actually know Tommy

Robinson?" the larger man asked casually, waiting for an answer which never came. Mick inched closer until the larger man started to tremble. He grabbed his smaller companion and said, "We have to go," and started pulling him down the hall.

"I thought you were going to show me something?" the smaller man whined.

"Later, stupid. Just shut up," the larger man said, and they scurried down the hall away from Mick and April.

April intertwined Mick's arm with hers, while looking up at him. "I've never seen anything like that. You never even said a word, and they ran. Amazing!" Mick just shrugged, and they went out into the cool Berlin night air.

Chapter 14

Letting Go

FBI Office, U.S. Embassy, Berlin Germany
0930 hours

The guard put the packages down to unlock the door. He briefly knocked first, as a polite gesture, and opened the door to Sasha's room. She was lounging on the couch watching television. He could see empty dishes on the table, so he knew that she had eaten. "I have some packages for you, Miss, left by Mr. Grundy. He said that you should have these before your meeting this morning which is in about an hour." He slid the packages into the room and nodded politely to her and closed the door. Sasha ignored him and continued to watch television.

1030 hours

Mick knocked softly on the door and then stepped back as the guard unlocked it. As soon as the door opened, Sasha rushed forward and embraced him. She looked up at him with a girlish grin and said, "You bought the clothes and shoes for me, didn't you?" He nodded that he did. "You have such good taste, Mick. You are going to be there this morning with me, aren't you?

"I'll be right there. We have a lot to discuss. Are you ready?"

"I'm ready to get out of this cage. As long as you are there with me, I can face anything." She took his arm and put it over her shoulder, so she could get closer to him. Escorted by the guard, they walked together, touching at the hips, toward the conference room where the group was already assembled. Around the table were seated, Ron Zeskie, April Chauncy and Elmer Septer, Station Chief of the FBI Berlin. When Sasha and Mick walked in arm in arm, some eyebrows were raised, especially those of April, and most certainly after the couple sat down directly across from her. Sasha leaned into Mick and surveyed the room like a captive animal from the protection of Mick's large shoulder.

Zeskie stacked his papers and cleared his throat. "Sasha Romanisky," he began. "You sought out Mick Grundy for a mission. We are here to listen, and I want you to repeat the reason we are here." He waited for her reply, with everyone present searching her face.

She straightened up and pulled back her hair. "I'm sure you know that I don't know the whole story. I was, and am, just a messenger. My instructions were to contact Mick and get him to a meeting with a superior. Other than that, you may know more about it than I do."

"Was your superior present in Tacoma with you," Zeskie asked, knowing the answer.

Sasha looked quickly at Mick, obviously not wanting to anger him before answering. "No, I was to get him to Germany, by any method." She looked at him again to discern his reaction. Mick remained passive and silent.

"Well, you accomplished your mission. Now what?" Zeskie inquired.

"I have a telephone number to call. After that, I wait for instructions," she said and again looked up at Mick.

"Assuming that your agency is embroiled in a faction struggle, do you realize that your life is at risk for many reasons?"

Sasha looked stunned as if she never considered that outcome a possibility. She put her hand to her mouth and looked at the faces around the table.

Mick patted her on her shoulder. "Sasha, it's like this. Your side may be finished with you or no longer trust you since you have been with us. If the other faction has gained control they will know that you are party to several of their agents being killed or arrested. They may even know that you personally shot one. There is only a slim chance that your contact will be there or will take care of you after you call. Another problem is that we may not agree with rendering any assistance in your people's internal struggle." When he finished, she slumped, pressing her face against the table, sobbing while leaning against Mick.

Elmer Septer spoke up, "We are not pressing charges against you, so after this conference is over, you are to leave the building." Mick glanced up at

April after noticing the harsh tone from her superior. He could detect the satisfaction in her eyes. April would not care in the least if Sasha would disappear forever.

Zeskie said, "We are ready to extend cover to you, Sasha, if you choose to formally defect. Other than that, you have to take your chances, I'm afraid.

Sasha held up her head proudly, while streaming tears. "I want to do my duty as a Russian who loves her motherland. Of course, I will make the call, if Mick is there with me. Whatever happens to me is my fate, after all.

Mick held her close and said, "And it seems to be my fate to accompany you into what will unfold. I will be with you."

Chapter 15

The Call

The Westin Grand Berlin
Friedrichstrasse
1300 hours

Mick chose a large hotel for Sasha's call, because a quick exit would be easier in case things went bad. They both agreed that a public telephone should be used to prevent her Russian contact from easily tracing them after the call was made. They found a bank of telephones off of the main lobby.

"Well, Sasha, this is the time and place. Make the call," Mick said.

"Do I tell them that you are beside me?"

"Of course. Tell them. I have to agree to any meeting place, however."

Nervously, she picked up the receiver and punched in the numbers. Mick heard the phone click as the other party picked it up. *"Этот Sasha. Я закончил мою миссию и жду инструкции."* ["This is Sasha. I have completed my mission and await instructions."] She shrugged her shoulders at Mick and waited for a response from the phone. The seconds ticked by while they both stood and looked at each other and the phone.

She was about to hang up when the phone clicked again, and a voice said, "We have been waiting for you. Do you possess the item?"

"Yes. He is right here beside me. He is willing to meet with you."

There was another lengthy delay, and then the voice came back and said, "Tell us where you are, and we will come get you."

Mick was listening and waved his finger back and forth to indicate no. Sasha told the party that Mick Grundy would not agree to a pick up. She listened and then extended the phone to him. "He wants to talk with you."

"Grundy," Mick said.

"Наконец, знаменитый Мик Грундай. Мы очень интересуемся тем, чтобы говорить с Вами. Так как мы не можем подобрать Вас, что является вашими предложениями?" ["At last, the famous Mick Grundy. We are very interested in talking to you. Since we can't pick you up, what are your suggestions?"]

"The Jewish Museum, Lindenstrase, two hours from now."

There was a long silence, and then the voice said, "Done," in perfect English.

Mick hung up the phone and, pulling her to her feet, said, "Come, we have to get there before they do." It was a short cab ride to the Museum, and as Mick remembered, there was high level security in position, including a metal scanner for patrons. While outside, he dialed Zeskie who picked right up.

"Zeskie, I need to get into the Jewish Museum for this meeting, and I want to bypass security. Can you help?"

"Are you carrying the IDs that you were given yesterday?" he asked.

"Yes, I have them."

"Pull out the one for M. Sorenson from INTERPOL and pin it to your chest. If that causes a problem, call me back." Zeskie disconnected without Mick's reply.

As instructed, Mick and Sasha approached the security guard with the badge and ID exposed, and as Zeskie predicted, they were waved on past with a smile. Mick motioned to the guard and said, *"Lassen Sie sich nicht jemand anderes in ohne Waffen zu überprüfen. Verstehen Sie?"* ["Don't let anyone else in without a weapon check. Do you understand?"] The guard gladly agreed, and they continued into the exhibit. They strolled arm in arm and pretended to look at the often horrible images from the war years. Mick was constantly scanning for threats, but Sasha appeared relaxed and smiled at him often. The two hours went by, and there was no sign of their contact. Mick began to imagine that perhaps Sasha's fellow agent was waiting for them to emerge outside, where superior forces could be ready for ambush. A small elderly man approached them with nodding and smiles, leaning on a cane and walking with a decided limp. He was wearing a yarmulke and was clearly Jewish. When he got close, he reached into his jacket and produced a small earpiece.

"I am instructed to tell you that this is your

contact." He placed the item in Mick's hand and shuffled away, talking to himself.

Mick put the piece into his ear and said, "Go ahead, I'm listening."

A deep voice appeared in his ear in Russian-accented English, "We talk at last, Mick Grundy. This is Alexander Sinitsin. My agent, Sasha, deserves a lot of credit for making this possible. My assurances that you have nothing to fear from me. I know your history and respect it, but I am not your enemy. The death of your dear wife was not sanctioned by me, and I personally have never sent agents to harm you. Now that that is behind us, we can proceed. Because you are our devoted enemy, you are the person that I can most trust. You could never be turned. We have a problem in Russia and, therefore, so does America. There are people rising to power who are dedicated to the destruction of the West by any means. They are using fanatical proxies in the Middle East to cause problems and unite around the banner of Islam. The Islamists are seeding your society with maniacs, and the movement is a rising force for you to deal with abroad and at home. They will not hesitate to use a nuclear device against you if they get one, and some Russians are making sure that they do. Russia blocks restraint at the level of the United Nations, while shipping supplies and technology to the third world as fast as possible. My own motherland is supplying missiles which will be modified for greater range in a short period. We provide material support and instructions on how to use these weapons. It is national insanity. Russia is surrounded on our southern borders by Islam which makes us more at risk than America. If the Islamists are successful with their plans of unification of a broad area, Russia will feel it first. I cannot let that happen and neither can you. We can't deal with your government, because your politicians, those presently in power, only seek reelection and getting the vote from those who think they have the most to gain but actually have the most to lose. Your country also is running itself into the mire. Someone has to act, and I hope that you will want to be a part of it."

Mick reflected for a moment and said, "I have heard all of this before. Not everyone in the U.S. is stupid, but I admit we have more idiots than our fair share. Exactly what role do you expect me to have?"

"Simply put, we must kill Anatoly Baranov, because his ideas are poison to reason. With him out of the way, there is some chance that I can get our President to see the truth."

Mick said, "When you say 'we must kill,' you really mean 'Mick Grundy must kill,' don't you?'

"No, I meant we when I said it," the deep voice answered.

"Then, what you want is for Mick Grundy to take the blame for the assassination. After all, I am already widely despised and hunted by your people, so what difference could another killing make?" There was no response from Sinitsin, if that indeed was him speaking. Mick continued, "I also realize that you will kill me and claim that you got one of Russia's enemies in order to get full benefit from the death of Baranov. To sum it up, it doesn't matter if I actually help to kill or actually kill Baranov. Either way, I get to be dead in the end."

Sinitsin sighed, "My friend, your experience has made you see the worst in people and outcomes. I want to come back into the light. The way I see it, after the positive changes which will come after Baranov's removal, Mick Grundy will become a hero of the Russian people. I certainly will see it that way. If you would allow yourself to be accompanied by some of my agents, we may be able to meet face to face, and you can gauge my sincerity with your own eyes."

Mick said, "I can't trust your people enough to allow myself to be taken in. You don't even trust your people. Another thing, Sinitsin, Russians rightly pride themselves in producing the world's best trained covert operatives. Get one of them to do the job."

"What if I told you that I have both written proof and recordings of Baranov ordering the attempted assassination of you which caused the death of your wife? I also can provide the name and location of the female agent who planted the bomb. Would you be interested in retaliation? I would if I were you. Baranov is also the one who continues to hunt you and will continue to do so until they succeed. Tell me now what you have to lose in joining with me? Russia and America are natural allies. If we can just work together to change the course of history, our nations, for once, may be unified. If we all die in the struggle, at least we tried."

Mick answered, "Sinitsin, either you are a great man or a great huckster. I have to talk this over with my superiors, so I am unwilling to be taken to you just yet. Also, I refuse to be taken into Russia under any conditions. If I do this for you, it must be outside of your borders, and I want to see the proof you offered first."

Sinitsin chuckled, "There is a good chance that Baranov will travel your direction soon. I am still collecting bits and pieces, but something is in the works. I suggest that Sasha be the go-between, because you two seem to have built some trust for one another. When you decide, let her set up the meeting. I need not point out that Baranov's people will kill her on sight if they find her. You must keep her safe, but at the same time, she must have freedom of movement. If you don't mind, you can give her the earpiece so I can give her instructions."

Mick pulled the device from his ear and helped Sasha position it in hers. He could tell by her expression that Sinitsin was telling her that Mick Grundy was willing to work with him. Whatever else she was told made her stare blankly into space and nod. When the conversation was complete, she pulled the device from her ear and stamped it into fragments against the stone floor.

"Now, you and I are real partners, Mick!" she said. "I want to make love to you right away. The tension is killing me, and you are all I think about." She started looking around the museum as if she were looking for a quiet corner or small room.

"No, Sasha, not here and not now. We have a lot to

do. The first thing is to get away from this place, alive. They know where we are, and I don't like it. When we try to leave, we are targets. I still don't trust anyone on your side. If Sinitsin gets the proof to me and I verify it, then maybe I will change my mind, but until then, we both would be wise to stay in the shadows."

Sasha frowned, "I thought that you understood that my side is not trying to kill you. If anyone is out there, they are friends, and we have nothing to worry about. We can just walk out the door."

"Even if what you say is true, did you consider that one of Baranov's men may have infiltrated Sinitsin's group? If that were true, we would be eliminated before we have a chance to go after Baranov. Don't trust anyone Sasha."

She pulled up close to him and pressed her breasts into his lower chest. "Can I trust you, Mick?"

"You can trust me. The question is can I trust you?" Mick asked, hugging her in return. After a quiet moment, Mick looked around and said, "I have an idea how to get out of here." He found his phone and dialed a number.

"I'm trying to reach Ron Zeskie," he said into the phone.

After a moment a voice said, "Zeskie here."

"I am with Sasha, and we are at the Jewish Museum. I have some concerns that someone may be waiting for us to go outside, and we need cover. A plan came to me that includes someone picking us up right outside the building in about ten minutes. Whoever comes should be alert for snipers.

"Wait, I get it. You are going to pull the fire alarm trick, aren't you?" Zeskie asked.

"Well, yes. You have a better idea?"

"Way better. Just wait inside the main door but out of sight. Should take less than ten minutes. You will know help when you see it."

The screech of tires outside was repeated twice. After a moment, two large men came through the door looking around intently. They were dressed in suits but looked more like bodybuilders in clothes too tight. One of the men spotted Mick and Sasha and came forward.

"You Grundy?" he said in a gruff voice. The man saw that Mick's hand was behind his back, probably with his pistol in it. "We are here to escort you outside. Don't shoot me, please." He pulled his ID slowly out of his jacket which said, "Agent Buddy Farmer, U.S. Secret Service."

"Let's go," Mick said and put his arm around Sasha's waist. They went out after the two large agents, and Mick could spot several others scattered outside scanning the horizon and pedestrians. As soon as they got in the big black SUV, the doors closed, and it accelerated briskly into traffic, followed by two others.

"Where to, sir?" one of the agents asked.

"I'm going back to the Embassy. Sasha?"

"Mick. Your phone. Can it be traced?"

"Not by anyone outside of the CIA."

Sasha had a far away look in her eyes, then started to tear. She looked grieved, and her lip trembled just a little. "I have to get out and trust that we were talking to my people back there. If you never hear from me again, you will know that I was wrong, and you should get away from here as fast as possible."

Mick reached into his pocket and pulled a large wad of euros out. "Take this. It might help you protect yourself a little before you contact them again. If you get cold feet, Zeskie has offered you asylum in the U.S. Should you want to give up this spy business, I will go back with you to be sure you are safe somewhere where they can't get you."

"Mick, if you will go back with me and stay with me forever, I will do anything you ever wanted, because I want more than anything to be with you. I have never met any man like you before and if anything happens to you because of me, I don't want to live any longer." She started to weep openly and clung to him and buried her face in his coat. The Secret Service agents in the car tried to look the other way.

"No, Sasha, I can't promise that I could stay with you. You already know that I am attracted to you and that I feel protective of you, but you couldn't stay out of view with me present. They would find us both eventually. I want to stay here and see what comes next. You are free to leave and live a long happy life somewhere where you can find peace."

She straightened up and wiped her eyes, her face becoming hard. "You will please give me your number so I can contact you."

Mick borrowed a pen from one of the agents and wrote his telephone number on the skin of her leg above the knee. "You don't have to do this, Sasha. I can make contact with them myself from now on."

"They won't trust you. You have killed too many Russians. I have to do it. No one else can. Tell the driver to stop here, and let me out," she said staring straight ahead, avoiding Mick's eyes. The vehicle jerked to a stop, idling. Sasha spun around to Mick and gave him a passionate kiss on the lips, then opened the door and walked away without looking back. Mick could taste the lipstick mixed with her tears. He almost called her back and watched as she slowly merged with other people and then was out of sight.

"Woman who looks like that and loves you too. Wow. I don't know any man but you, Grundy, who could watch her walk away. I know that I couldn't," one of the agents said.

"Embassy, guys," Mick ordered.

Chapter 15

Chapter 16

Picking Up The Package

FBI Office, U.S. Embassy, Berlin Germany
0930 hours

Zeskie snapped open his briefcase and reached for his coffee. Mick and April watched in silent amusement at his fussy and ritualistic preparations. He looked up and smiled at them. "I know what you are thinking. It's like a surgeon preparing for an operation. When I do it this way, I don't forget anything. I like to be orderly, and it often pays off."

April smiled at Mick who was across the table from her. He also had an amused smile on his face. Finally, Zeskie was ready to talk and looked up from his papers.

"Well, Mick, we heard most of what you said on the call but not the other side, of course. Want to fill us in on what we missed?"

Mick began, "The voice identified himself as Sinitsin and had a spiel about all the reasons that everyone should need to eliminate Baranov. He said that Baranov was the one who ordered me to be killed and is, therefore, responsible for Anna's death and said he would provide proof. He recanted all the world's problems and more or less said that getting rid of Baranov would help straighten us all out."

April said, "Did you buy it?"

Mick shrugged, "He seemed sincere on the phone, but I can't be sure that he even was Sinitsin, much less what he said was true. I am not sure, that even if what he said was true, that killing Baranov would benefit our side. What about it, Ron; what do you think?"

"As you are aware, there is a known conflict between factions in the Russian Intelligence Services. We have ample evidence of it. We don't have any direct or indirect contact with either Baranov or Sinitsin. We would lose if we pick the losing side and perhaps not gain much if we pick the winning side. As far as ordering the killing of Mick Grundy, well, that is a given after you dispatched some of their key people and personally gave them a black eye. The fact that it has gone on so long is a mystery. They normally just lick their wounds and try something else. There is something personal in it, but I don't have a clue at this time what it is."

"Where is your friend, Sasha?" April asked with narrowed eyes.

"She got out on the way back to be on her own. She is to connect with me by phone after she makes contact with her people. Could be, we will never see her again."

"Good, I don't trust her."

Zeskie shuffled his papers and cleared his throat. "April, about the two Russians the FBI took in Las

Vegas. I know that your people didn't get much from them, but after the CIA took them out of the country, we did squeeze them like a dry lemon. One of them, unfortunately, did not survive in our hands and died of natural causes. The other opened up after that and talked his head off. Seems he didn't know there was a struggle going on in his agency. He had heard of both Baranov and Sinitsin but had never seen either one in person. He had orders to kill Mick and to kill Sasha after she found Mick. From what he said, it appears that Sasha was cooperating with them under a master plan and was in constant contact. When he heard that Sasha had killed one of their own, he was furious. There is no doubt that she acted on her own initiative to save Mick. Whether that means that she is trustworthy to us remains to be seen. Someone evidently wants Mick to kill Baranov and doesn't want to do it themselves. Probably for obvious reasons."

Mick said, "That is about what both April and I thought. They sure don't mind throwing away some of their own, do they? Pretty well anything goes to accomplish their goals."

April looked surprised. "You mean that you suspected Sasha was just playing a role? I thought you were stricken with her and believed anything she said."

Mick smiled and said, "April, I trust you completely, and I sort of trust Zeskie, but I don't trust anyone else."

Zeskie leaned back and laughed, "I wouldn't trust me either, Mick."

Mick said, "'OK, Chief. Now what?"

"I am trying to get a handle on where Sinitsin and Baranov are, and I intend to trace their movements. We might as well get prepared if they come our way. There isn't much for you two to do right now, so go take some free time until we figure this out. One more thing, you both should be extra cautious out there and take your weapons with you at all times."

"Always," Mick agreed.

As they left the conference area, Mick said, "April, I want to go see someone in Stuttgart. Would you come with me? I am sure that you would enjoy the experience."

"I most certainly will go with you, Mick, but can you tell me who I will be meeting?"

"I have to make a couple of calls first, but if they are free, you will be able to meet my German family. They are all I have in the world, and they mean more to me than anything. I am ashamed that I haven't seen them in such a long time, but I am always afraid of bringing danger into their lives."

"This time is different?" she asked. "I would think the dangers right now are very high. They probably don't know about me, but your enemies are searching for you, and they know everything about you."

"All three of them are involved with the German BND, but I was instructed not to bring the Germans in on this case. I am unable to talk to them directly about the issues, but they may know already, because Germans are very careful and methodical. All I want is to see my family again. I can't leave

Germany without doing it."

"Mick, call them first and then decide. They may tell you what to do," April said and patted his arm.

They walked down to the cafeteria and brought two coffees back to a table, and Mick took out his phone.

"Triska! This is Mick!" he said. Mick rarely seemed happy, but April could see a broad smile break out. "Yes, dear, I am in Berlin! I hoped that we four could get together while I'm here, and I can make up for all the time since my last visit." He listened for a while and said, "I understand. No, I agree that I am probably being watched. That will be fine, dear. Is it all right if I bring my partner to meet you? No, she is my professional partner, not the other kind. Yes. Nine in the morning? We will be waiting. Goodbye, love."

April raised her eyebrows waiting for the answer to a question she didn't have to ask.

"She didn't say so, but she apparently knows what is going on. She and her grandson, my brother-in-law, are going to come to the BND Headquarters in Berlin tonight, and she will send a car to get us and take us over there in the morning."

"Who, exactly, is Triska?" April asked.

"Triska was Anna's paternal grandmother. She is an old spy who has been active since the early Cold War. It seems that she always knows what is going on, and she speaks several languages fluently. She can find out everything about you in a few moments of casual questions. I dearly love her and so will you."

April asked, "You said the four of us. Who are the

others?"

"There is Kurt, my brother-in-law. He has just finished college and was also my motorcycle buddy when I was here. Great guy. He has joined the spy business also, but I don't know what he is doing or exactly where he works now. We were very close for a while. Then there is my actual brother, half brother to be exact, and my only living relative as far as I know. He has a military background and had Special Forces training just like I did. Peter Koffman. He works for the BND also but officially is in the German Army. Last time I saw him, he was an *Oberst*. May even be higher ranked by now. We bonded the first time we saw each other but only found out our blood relationship much later and quite by accident." Mick unconsciously touched the side of his head where the bullet had struck remembering the event which had nearly killed him. He continued after a moment of thought. "There was a sample of my blood taken after an injury when I was admitted to a German Hospital. Typical Germans, they ran my DNA and found a match with Peter. We still don't know how it was possible."

"Same mother or same father?" April asked.

"The DNA says maternal." My mother was killed in the U.S. shortly after my birth in a car accident along with my father, or so the record shows. They were cremated, so no DNA. Zeskie said that they could have been working for the East German Communists and were a plant. It seems that my adoptive parents were also Communist plants and were also killed in a car accident. Since I don't believe in coincidence, there is more to the story, and some day I will know the facts and the truth. So you see, I have always been associated with the Russians in some fashion. Unfortunately for them, I am a loyal American."

"I can see that letting me meet your family is a great honor. There are no words to express how grateful I am, Mick." Moisture formed in her eyes, and she turned away from him to hide it.

"You are my first real partner, and you should know everything you can about me. I trust you with my life, why shouldn't I trust you with my family?" he said and reached out and put his hand on her shoulder.

Before April could answer, Mick's phone rang. He picked it out of his pocket and whispered, "It's Sasha."

"Hello, Sasha," he said quietly. After listening for a moment, he said, "I'll be there," and hung up.

"Don't tell me that she wants another meeting," April asked. There was both apprehension and loathing in her voice.

"Yes, this afternoon. She has an item for me. She didn't say anything about a meeting with anyone." He furrowed his brow and then punched in a number. "Zeskie, can you get me the loan of a fast motorcycle for this afternoon?"

"I'm afraid to ask why, Mick. As I remember, most of your rides end up with someone getting shot," Zeskie recalled. "Sure, I think I have a solution. Call you back."

April looked across at him with worry on her face. "What do you have to do, Mick?"

"I have to meet Sasha at the *Schwerbelastungskörper* and pick up an item."

"What is the... what did you call it?" she asked.

"The *Schwerbelastungskörper*. As I recall, it's some old concrete structure left over from the war. It's west of here about two miles," he said.

April took out her smartphone and looked it up. "Here it is. The English name is 'Heavy Load-Bearing Body.' Looks kind of evil from the photos."

Mick's phone rang again. "When do you have to go, Mick?" Zeskie asked.

"About an hour from now. I would like to get there early to scout it out. A motorcycle is best for quick in and out, and no one can follow me on a motorcycle."

"Well, I got a ride for you, and he will be in front in about thirty minutes. Please don't tear it up, or we will have to pay for it."

Thirty minutes later, Mick was waiting on the sidewalk outside the American Embassy when he heard the sound of a powerful four cylinder motorcycle approaching. The bike, painted bright white and red, pulled up sharply in front of him. The rider inspected him through his dark visor before he pulled off the helmet.

"Ihr Name Grundy?"

Mick nodded yes and waited for the man to get off and pull off his gloves. When he did, they shook hands.

"Müssen Sie auch Helm, Handschuhe und Jacke?" the rider asked. Mick smiled and nodded yes, and the man pulled off his jacket and handed all of his gear to Mick. "It's new. You will be careful to bring it

back, yes?" he said as he motioned to the bike which was still running.

Mick donned the outfit and pulled open the helmet visor, "I'll be as careful as they let me. I should be back in an hour. Will you wait?"

The man frowned, *"Nein. Sie können es so lange wie Sie es brauchen zu halten."* and walked away at a brisk pace.

Mick swung his leg over the bike and inspected it quickly. BMW S1000RR. Nice choice, he thought, then revved it up and jerked away from the curb, accelerating quickly into traffic. He worked the bike hard in traffic and made sure that no car could follow his path between lines of cars or his path over curbs and along sidewalks for short periods. He made a long circular approach toward his destination, keeping constant vigilance in the rear view mirrors, satisfied that he was alone. His target was just ahead at the corner of *General-Pape* and *Loewenhardtdamm*. Rolling by slowly, he looked it over discreetly as if he were just passing by. There was a small parking area, just behind an apartment complex, which had a good view of the massive concrete structure. The grounds were overgrown with small trees and weeds, and no one else was around. He smoothly glided back onto the small streets and rode around the block, keeping the structure just out of view. The neighborhood was mostly apartments near a complex of railroad tracks to the east of the *Schwerbelastungskörper*. A glance at his watch confirmed that the time for his rendezvous with Sasha was near. When he turned into the parking lot adjacent to the structure he saw her standing alone near the entrance. He looked around but saw no one else, then accelerated toward her and came to an abrupt stop on the sidewalk in front of her. She startled backward for an instant and then cocked her head to get a better look. Mick opened the helmet visor and smiled. There was no return smile as she walked by while reaching out, placing something into his open jacket pocket then continuing silently on her way. Twisting to watch her disappear down the path, he noticed that she never looked back at him. He twisted the throttle hard, applying all 186 horsepower to the rear wheel which shot him out of the parking lot as if out of a gun. The same procedure was followed across Berlin to avoid being tracked back to the American Embassy. He showed his badge at the entrance to the underground parking garage and was waved through by the armed Marine on duty. Parking the bike, he had another look at it before walking away. Just right for his needs here. He reminded himself to request that Zeskie keep it for him.

Chapter 17

Reunion

0700 hours

The next morning, he met April in the cafeteria for coffee. They were scheduled to be picked up in one hour by BND agents for their meeting with Mick's relatives. Mick was excited and happy, and he was relieved to see that April was bright and alert as well. Possibly, he hoped, she was interested in getting a glimpse of the other side of Mick. As they were sipping coffee and engaging in small talk, Zeskie came up and put his briefcase on the table. He yawned and stretched before asking, "Coffee any good this morning?"

They both chimed, "Good morning!" Zeskie rolled his eyes and said, "Well, I see that you both got more sleep than I did. Good morning to you both. I hear that you have an outing this morning, and I am happy for you. First things first, though." He snapped open his briefcase and sat down. He took out yet another stack of papers and sorted through them. "The memory chip supplied via Sasha was interesting. There is a large stack of documents here and all of them in Russian. I sent the lot to Langley last night. There is a short video made by the one and only Alexander Sinitsin. I verified that it is actually him on the recording. It is directed to you, so you have to see it yourself, but it is a replay of what you were already told. He is pleading for help to eliminate his rival, and he wants you to do it. The other items are interesting in another way," he said, pulling a stack of photo prints out of the briefcase and sliding them across the table.

Mick and April moved closer and went through the photos together. The first ones were curious old photographs of three different young women. Some shots were formal, some were of each holding a baby. Judging by the uniforms worn in the formal poses, the pictures were taken in East Germany during the Communist regime. Photos of several different men, paired with the women in the first group of pictures, smiled out from the past. The baby seemed to be the same in all the pictures. The last group was of Mick and April, from the moment of arrival in Berlin until yesterday, and included every place they had been together. There were photos of two residences that Mick recognized with a chill. One was the house of Jennifer and Jonnie in Tacoma, and the other was of Triska's apartment building in Stuttgart.

Mick put down the photos and said, "Those dirty sons of bitches. This is a threat, Zeskie. They are telling me that they will take out anyone connected to me if I don't cooperate."

"That's obvious, Mick. What do you make of the old photos from the commie era?" Zeskie inquired.

"I have never seen any of these people. Can the

CIA identify them?" Mick asked.

"We are having Langley process them right now, and we should have some answers by evening. The most important thing to understand at the moment is that April is in danger and so is Triska. You should alert the BND while you are there, and bring them into this." He turned to April, "My dear and favorite FBI Agent. You should be armed and alert at all times from now forward. It's always shocking to see the capabilities of the other side. They are resourceful, even masterful, at this game, and they are totally ruthless. I am anxious to know what an analysis of this material turns up, but given what we know right now, I can summarize as follows. They are determined to have Mick do an assassination for them, and they will plead with him, bribe him, or threaten him to do it. My bet is that they will liquidate him if and when he completes this mission for them and claim credit for doing in an enemy of the Russian state. We will see, perhaps, but my feeling is that the older photos are connected with Mick's parentage, and they are advising him that the truth of his origins are available if he is interested."

"You never should have taken this on, Mick," April said.

"It looks like I have had a destiny to get involved. I never had a choice. You do, April. You should go back home where your people can watch out for you. What would it accomplish if you get killed over here?"

"I have been assigned to this mission and to you, and I won't let it go, because I care about both. Get used to it. I am here to stay until it is over, one way or the other."

Zeskie smiled, "Yes, true partnership. Or is it true love? You two are a great team, because you really care about each other. The question for each of you is, can you live with yourself if your partner is killed?"

"No," Mick said. "But I'm not going to let it happen. Let's go, April, they'll be waiting. Later, Zeskie." Mick stood and took April's arm and led the way to the black limousine waiting and idling at the curb.

As they approached, the passenger door opened, and a large man dressed in a black jumpsuit emerged smiling. He opened the rear door for them and chirped, "Brother! It is *wunderbar* to see you again!" He spread his large arms and wrapped Mick in them and picked him off his feet. "So happy am I to see you again!"

When he put Mick back down, Mick patted him affectionately on the cheek, "I am also happy to see you again, Peter. Sorry it's been so long." Mick turned and gestured toward April and remarked, "I want to introduce my partner, Special Agent April Chauncy of the FBI. Don't try and pick her up, or she may shoot you!"

Peter drew himself up to rigid attention and clicked his heels and bowed at the waist while extending his hand to her. "*Oberst* Peter Koffman, at your service. *Mein Gott*, you are beautiful." He smiled broadly at her and shook his head in amazement. "Mick, my partner looks like a goat. You are very fortunate, I must say." He waved at the open car door, and they all piled into the ample back seat. April sat between the two men but soon wished that she would have been allowed on the outside. Mick and Peter carried on an active conversation just above her head. She constantly had to duck hand gestures which were a similar emphasis of speech of both men.

"Still *Oberst*, Peter?" Mick questioned with a smile.

"Ya," he answered. "I may never make *Brigadegeneral* in this life." He sighed. "Always the same for me. We chase the bad ones, and we are allowed to shoot some of them from time to time, but we never get to blow them up like the Americans do." He sighed again. "Are you here on another dangerous mission, Mick?"

"I'm afraid that the answer is yes. We both are. I was just instructed to bring your people in, and when we arrive at the BND, I want you to arrange a meeting so that I can inform your side what is going on."

Peter frowned and looked serious for the first time. "I will do that, Mick. You have your reunion over lunch, and I will set up something for the early afternoon."

"Some of it concerns you and them, Peter, and I want you there for lunch also." The serious tone from Mick did not go unnoticed. "Are you married yet, Peter?" Mick asked.

"*Nein*. But I am seeing Brigitte only now. You remember the Director's personal secretary, don't you?"

Mick recalled a memory of a stunning and curvy

blond in a tight skirt and blouse. "Yes, I believe I remember her. Are you sure that you are mature enough for her?"

Peter laughed, "Yes, Mick, that is the one. Are you going to marry this FBI agent?"

"Wait a minute, you two. I am here between you, and you ignore me and then say something like that. I am getting tired of it. From now on, you may pass your questions through me first," April said in mock anger.

"Very well, Special Agent Chauncy," Peter said. "Would you please ask the distinguished gentleman on your left if he is going to marry you and then report his answer back to me?" Peter had a hard time containing his laughter which erupted when April poked him in the ribs with her elbow.

April said, "Now, I have some questions. Which one of you is the older brother? When you answer, I will expect more maturity from that one."

The two men looked serious for a moment and then both shrugged. Clearly, they didn't know.

The car took a hard turn and entered a dark cavern. They had arrived at the *Bundesnachrichtendienst*, the German Intelligence Agency, and when the door opened, several heavily armed guards were in view.

When they emerged from the car, a well-dressed man with a smile approached them. He was trim and wore an expensively tailored suit and mirror-polished black shoes. He had a practiced smile and a booming voice. "My dear friends, welcome to *Hauptquartier*. My name is Herbert Gruber, and I would like to be your personal guide this morning. I have some identity badges for you to wear while you are here, and unfortunately, we have to hold your weapons while in this building. You may give them to my assistant, and we will be sure to return them when you exit."

Mick hesitated and held Gruber in a withering stare until Peter tapped him and whispered, "No problem, Mick. This is procedure, and you must comply." Mick and April reluctantly gave up their weapons and were led through a metal detector before being whisked to the elevator bank by the able Gruber.

"Our Director is Gunther Weisman, and we will report to his office at once. He is expecting you," Gruber said with his solicitous smile. Hearing the name, Mick shot a glance at Peter who nodded that this was the same one indeed.

Mick had encountered Weisman years ago on his first trip to the BND offices in Stuttgart. Weisman had graciously allowed Anna and Mick to have their wedding right there, in the BND chapel, and afterward, sent them away on their honeymoon covered by BND field agents who were to shadow them and protect against any attack by the Russians. Anna was killed less than twenty-four hours later by a bomb which also nearly killed Mick. The entire event remained crisply fresh in his memory as it always will be as long as he lived. Wedding Anna was the greatest day of his life and losing her was the worst day. Since that event, he never recovered from the loss and was aware that he was hollow inside. He had never been with a woman before or since Anna. To do so would spoil what little memory of her that he had left to hold him together. In Mick's view, he had died that day, at least part of him had. He was no longer afraid of death, and for a long time, his only reason for living was revenge. You can only be driven by hate for so long, and over time, he found people that he could again care about. Being in this building and seeing Gunther Weisman would again rekindle all the old violence in him. Fate had stepped in, as it usually does, and now the future was being laid down before him like a pair of steel rails heading into the distance.

The posh elevator door popped open on the top floor, and standing in the hall in front of the elevator was Gunther Weisman. As always, he was impeccably attired in a dark pinstripe suit and bright silk tie. He fixed Mick's eyes in his gaze and moved forward with his hand extended. His practiced smile was replaced by a serious and concerned look.

"My dear Mick Grundy. At last we meet again," he said as he held Mick's hand tightly with both of his and continued to unblinkingly look him in the eyes.

"It is good to see you again also, Director Weisman," Mick said. "I see that your career has continued to propel you to the top. Congratulations."

"Mick," he stumbled. "I..."

Mick released his hand from Weisman's grip and patted him on his shoulder. "No, please don't apologize, Director. You did what you had to do. The Russians tricked us all. They never stop. That is why I'm back again, and we have a lot to discuss. By the way, I want to introduce my partner," Mick said and turned to look at April standing beside him.

Director Weisman smiled broadly at April and said, "I expect that you are FBI Special Agent April Chauncy. I am Gunther Weisman, and on behalf of the BND, I want to extend every courtesy to you both. I hope you will not be offended when I say that you are far more attractive in person than in your photographs."

"Thank you, Director Weisman. I am privileged to be here this morning, and I would like to offer any assistance that my agency can provide," April said and took the Director's hand in a very firm shake. They all filed into the Director's private conference room which was carpeted in a muted red. The table and walls were of highly-figured and polished gleaming walnut. Two very attractive female assistants were present, who helped seat everyone in a predetermined chair.

Director Weisman smiled around the table and said, "It seems that most of us have done this before," while he opened the files placed before him by his assistant. "I have some documents which were rushed over just now from your inimitable Ron Zeskie. I am informed that other documents will follow as the CIA finishes with their analysis. After brief study, I want to make something very clear. The German government will not be a party to assassination. At this moment in history, I don't believe that your government will agree to it either. Yes, we have done it in the past and may well do it again, but there isn't enough provocation in this matter for us to risk a return to the Cold War." He looked directly at Mick to be sure his point was made. "However, I don't think we have a problem with an individual acting on his or her own given sufficient reason and...enough reliable proof. That is the stickler in this issue. Documents which are original may be analyzed but reproductions cannot. Each and every one that was placed on the memory chip and delivered to you could be fake. There is no way that we can verify them. Ultimately, you, Mick, must decide what course of action to take based on your impulses. As far as this office is concerned, you may do anything you wish in Germany without repercussions as long as no innocent German citizen is harmed. *Oberst* Koffman is hereby authorized to provide you with assistance of any kind you may need. As far as the implied threat against Triska, they are going to regret bringing her into this, and we are initiating painful remedies at this moment. When they realize what a hornet's nest they have opened, we should have no more problems with them. At least until next time, that is."

"Sir, what do your people make of the other photographs? I mean the East Germans and the baby?"

"Just looking at them reminds me of the sad time we Germans had for so long with the fanatics the Soviets installed in the *Ministerium für Staatssicherheit.* You might remember this organization as the Stasi. We have to open the old and immense paper files and dig through them by hand. It could take months or longer to run these photos down without knowing any names. It's obvious that the photos were placed to give you hope of discovering your past. Who knows? On this, they might actually be supplying a real lead. Or not." He shrugged. "I am sure that you know the risks to yourself, Mick. Do you also intend for your beautiful partner to share the same risks?"

"I'll answer that, Mick," said April. "Given the assurances you just gave Mick, I am sure that it is permitted that I may return deadly force with deadly force?" The Director blinked affirmative. "Remember, my friends, that I also do this for a living. I take any risks on myself, and I don't need Mick's permission to do so."

"Well said, Special Agent Chauncy," *Oberst* Koffman interrupted. "This is a different operating environment than the U.S. The enemy seems to feel that they can get by with more here than you are used to seeing in the States. Your partner has exhibited an uncanny ability to perceive danger before it arrives. Please trust his judgment and intuition."

April didn't respond, and there was a moment of uncomfortable silence. Director Weisman interjected, "Well, next on the agenda is a happy reunion, long overdue, and I am joyed to be party to it. Since our business here is concluded for now, I would like to play host and invite all of you to stay here and have lunch with me. Triska and Kurt are on their way up, and lunch will be served shortly." He stood and motioned that the door should open, and when it did, it opened to reveal a short compact grey-haired woman standing arm in arm with a tall slender young man who wore a shock of unruly brown hair. Both had broad smiles and came into the room excitedly. Mick got up quickly and rushed to embrace them both. April noticed that Mick brushed away a tear or two, and the three danced around the room locked in an extended embrace. Director Weisman was beaming and applauded the joyous scene.

Mick took both by the hand and led them to April's chair. She rose to greet them with a smile and offer of handshake. "You must be Triska," she said as she took the old lady's small hand in hers. She could see through the smile that Triska was sizing her up with a couple of discreet glances.

"Don't be disarmed by her size and age, April," Mick said over Triska's shoulder. "She is a clever old spy and not to be underestimated." He laughed at his own humor and slapped his brother-in-law, Kurt, on the shoulder.

"Mick! Seriously, this is your partner?" Kurt asked in disbelieve when he was introduced to April.

"Yes, Kurt," Mick answered. "I know that you are concerned to know how I can stand it, but remember that I was in the U.S. Army, and they taught us to never complain."

April rolled her eyes and said, "Glad to meet you also, Kurt." As they sat down, Triska was seated across from April, and they were able to converse eye to eye. April was warned by Mick previously about Triska's ability to interrogate efficiently without seeming to, and the warning was well-taken. Triska was able to keep the conversation seemingly innocent but gradually picked her way across April's mind, and if she had enough time, she would eventually discover every detail of her life. April was thankful when the table's conversation finally turned to Mick's relationship to Peter Koffman.

"You mean to say that neither one of you has had the time or interest to discover your roots?" Director Weisman asked both of them with sincere incongruity. "I think that given what is now happening with the Russians, we and you need to know the truth and the facts as it may have bearing on this affair."

Mick said, "With respect, Director. My records in the States are a dead end. Both sets of parents were killed in auto accidents. Mr. Zeskie has suggested that my adoptive parents were East German or Russian spies, and he went farther to speculate that my original parents are also suspected. There is nothing I can do about the utter lack of information but wonder." He looked over at Peter Koffman to see if he could add anything.

Peter nodded agreement with his brother. "I have seen the DNA evidence myself, and indeed, we are half brothers with differing fathers. I was raised by loving parents, who both have since passed away. I was never told that I was adopted. After discovering Mick's relationship to me, I had an examination done from blood samples retained by our excellent medical facilities and discovered that I must have been adopted, because my parents were not my biological parents. I too must confess that I don't know my origins, and just like my brother over there, I only have one living person in the world that I know is related to me."

"This is unacceptable," Director Weisman snarled. "You both work for the world's best intelligence agencies, and you are from the two most first world of first world countries. We can do better. Peter, let me guess, your parents were likely killed in an auto accident?"

"Ja, Herr Director," Peter acknowledged somewhat sheepishly.

The Director was reddening in the face as he turned this over. "Well, there it is. This case is all under us and all around us. Here we are together seemingly not by accident but as if under Divine guidance. It is our destiny to solve this riddle, and we must do it quickly. Triska, do you have anything to add from your long knowledge of East German Stasi meddling in human affairs?"

Triska frowned and drew herself up. "I know nothing of this case, and if it was done by Stasi, it would have been a very secret operation. This is the kind of thing that they were doing...creation of identities and planting future secret agents to be called on later in life. The Russians, or forgive me, the Soviets, were the puppet masters of the puppet masters and on whom, ultimately, the responsibility must rest. The records are available to us, because we retained all the state records when the Iron Curtain fell, but they are vast and contain many square kilometers of data. To me, the origin of these two men makes no difference. They are brave and loyal and have proven themselves over and over. I don't care where they came from, and I am proud to have them here beside us today."

Mick offered, "The photographs may yet tell a story, but I will have to meet with Alexander Sinitsin to get the rest of it. It seems that for many reasons, this meeting will happen, and what comes next is guesswork."

The early afternoon was spent in friendship with several conversations happening at the same time. The BND spared no expense and had a catered lunch provided in shifts. There was an assortment of flavored Schnaps available and also plenty of good dark German beer. Mick noticed that Kurt was mesmerized by April and hung on her every word. She occasionally glanced at Mick to let him know that she wanted to get away from Kurt, but Mick just smiled at her and was obviously enjoying her celebrity.

Triska pulled on the sleeve of Director Weisman and asked, "Do you know anything about gunfire near my apartment in Stuttgart last night when we were about to leave?"

Weisman gave her his plastic grin and said, "It was reported that two individuals were shot in your neighborhood resisting arrest after an attempt was made to detain them."

"Ooh," Triska said with mock surprise. She put her hand to her mouth briefly. "I do hope they weren't seriously injured."

"Unfortunately, they didn't survive for questioning. Hopefully, the matter is closed," he said.

"One more thing, Director?" she asked pleasantly.

He looked down at her knowing that Triska would never let anything go easily. "From the conversations this morning, I gathered that we were only informed this very morning about the indirect threat to me. Given the action near my apartment last night, it seems to imply that there was some prior knowledge. Can you clarify this for me?" She looked sweetly up at him, and he knew that this old devil was still up to her tricks.

"As you know, my dear Triska, we always try to keep up with events and to use interception when possible. Is there a complaint you have about our efforts to keep you safe?" Director Weisman answered in a patronizing way.

"No, my sweet Director. Thank you for always looking after me. I would hope that you could see that I will be better informed about any impending risks, and I also hope that you are able to see that our friends in the CIA don't hear about it, because there could be some uncomfortable questions raised."

"Point well taken, Triska," he said.

Chapter 18

An Astonishing Admission

FBI Office, U.S. Embassy, Berlin Germany
1730 hours

Zeskie looked tired when he pulled back his chair and plopped down his scruffy briefcase. "Greetings, you two. Did your party over there make you happy?"

Mick and April had been waiting for him for a half-hour in his private office and were not in the best of moods. "You know that we are always happy, Zeskie. What's up?" Mick inquired.

"Our people at Langley said the same thing as the Germans. Interesting documents, but no conclusion as to validity. The photos are more interesting. Our people are confidently sure that the adult males in the photos are of Alexander Sinitsin and Anatoly Baranov. They both were stationed in East Germany during the Cold War. The females pictured are unknown to us. The infant..." Zeskie paused and looked at Mick to see if he was ready for the rest. "The infant's face was analyzed by some experimental facial recognition software that they are playing with. The conclusion, after aging the face and a lot of guesswork, is that the infant is Mick Grundy."

Down deep, Mick had suspected as much, but it was still a blow having it said out loud. His mind reeled to places that he didn't want it to go. He became confused, losing his focus. April reached out and placed her hand over his clenched fist, and the warmth of her touch spread out to the rest of his body giving him an island to cling to. Mostly, he wanted to blurt out that it wasn't true, at the same time feeling the need to run outside the building to get his breath. He wanted any escape from the facts being presented to him, because the history he had invented for himself was far better than truth. Sadly, he couldn't hide or pretend any longer, because he was about to find out who he really was.

April frowned and said, "What does this mean, Ron?"

"It doesn't mean a damn thing. What we have identified here are some old photographs. We haven't proved any relationships or clarified a chain of events. Photographs can come from anywhere and even they can be faked. All we know is what they want us to think, not what actually is. They are putting out a story line backed up by documents and photographs. Eventually, and with the BND's help, we will have a more accurate portrait of past events, but it will take additional time that Mick doesn't have."

"Something else happen, Zeskie?" Mick asked, as from a slumber.

Zeskie reached into his pocket and slid an

envelope across the table to Mick. "This came about an hour ago. The messenger left it with a Marine guard outside the Embassy gate. We identified the messenger as Sasha but made no effort to retain her."

Mick picked up the tattered envelope which was marked with "MG" in pencil on the outside. He pulled the letter out and saw that it was handwritten, also in pencil. "Tonight at 10:00, same place. Be careful. Sasha," was written in a loose scrawl in a diagonal across the paper. Mick glanced at his watch, then at April and Zeskie. "You read it, Zeskie?" he asked.

"As CIA station chief, I read all incoming mail. Yes, I read it. Are you going?"

"This is the meeting we have been waiting for. Yeah, I'm going. I know you will send a squad over there, Zeskie, but don't bother. They will expect it, and, I'm sure, be ready with an alternative. They want this meeting very badly so I won't be harmed, because they want me alive to carry out their plans. Just let me go it alone. That way all you have to lose is one man who was always doomed anyhow."

"I refuse to let you do this by yourself!" April said in a shout. "I am going. Get used to it."

"You are not going, April. If a squad of Marines isn't enough, then how could you do anything but get hurt. I can't think about your safety as well as my own. You are not going, and that is final." After he spoke, he realized that he had spoken harshly to her, and he turned to make an apology but was distracted by Zeskie.

"Just so you both know, we will have a team of

four Marine snipers getting in position about now. If we see any, and I mean any, hostile intent, they will open fire. They are using a blue laser. Watch for the spots," Zeskie said. He knew that Mick Grundy understood that he meant the small targeting spot used to light up the bullet strike area.

2130 hours

Mick swung his leg over the purring motorcycle and pulled on his helmet and gloves. He checked his back one more time for his 45 caliber pistol and then took one last look at April and Zeskie. A quick wave and he gunned the bike up the slope toward the street.

It felt good letting a fast motorcycle whisk him through the dark streets. He always had the feeling of isolation while riding a motorcycle through the night air. A sort of being invisible feeling. He remembered how much he loved riding and began to relax. The bike was fast, and he darted around cars and then hard around the corners, putting his knee to the street, then accelerating hard while the bike slowly regained the vertical. Too quickly, he reached his destination. By now the landmarks were familiar, and he rode slowly into the parking lot near the monument of concrete. He pulled up to the curb and let the bike idle, remaining astride. No one was around, and the monument loomed darkly in the distance like a gigantic tombstone marking the passing of the Nazi era. He noticed something which made him look down. When he did, a brief and intense blue dot appeared and disappeared from his chest. They were telling him that he was covered. The Marines had arrived and were ready.

They all waited in silence. Mick switched off the bike and stood watching the cars come and go, passing by on the nearby street. The time went from 1000 to 1030 and still no action. They continued to wait. A car turned into the parking lot and moved slowly forward in near silence. As the car approached, Mick could see that it was a black Mercedes limousine. It pulled up behind the motorcycle, and the rear door opened. Mick didn't move and watched the car in silence. A hand stuck out the back and waved to him to come toward the car. When he continued to stand in place, a voice in Russian-accented English called out, "Come, Mick Grundy, come. We talk now." Mick ignored the call and waited in position. Finally, a dark shape emerged from the car and came toward him. The man coming forward was blocky and shorter than Mick and seemed more to amble along rather than walk. As he got closer, Mick recognized the face of Alexander Sinitsin. The man stuck out his hand for a shake, but Mick stood still with his hands in his pockets.

"Okay, Mick Grundy, we are not friends. I know this. We have much to discuss. Can you get in the car so that we can talk more quiet? Yes?"

"I'm comfortable talking right here. I don't like getting into dark cars in the middle of the night."

"Don't be silly, my friend. If I wanted to shoot you, I could do it at any time just by raising my hand," Sinitsin boasted.

"Prove it," Mick suggested.

Sinitsin shrugged, chuckled and raised his little finger. Nothing happened. He kept looking at Mick's chest for something and seemed to show some surprise.

"You mean, like this?" Mick said and raised his little finger. Sinitsin's chest glowed with blue dots which hovered like bright little bees looking for a place to land. "U.S. Marines. They never miss," Mick bragged.

"Okay, my friend, you win. Only I don't intend you any harm. Since you have the advantage, you may as well sit in my car so we can discuss."

"Have your driver roll down all the windows, and I will," Mick said. Sinitsin made a rolling gesture to the driver, and soon the windows dropped around the car. They both got in.

"We shall start anew. I am Alexander Sinitsin as you obviously know. By now you know that I want you to kill our mutual enemy, and you know most of the reasons. He is your enemy and has been hunting you since birth. Baranov will never stop until you are dead, and the real reason is to get at me. You, by yourself, are nothing to him, but as my son, you are his enemy." He stopped and watched Mick's face but could see no flicker of emotion or even that he had heard the dramatic statement. "I have to admit, the Americans trained you to be as hard a man as I have ever seen. I am proud to call you my own, my son." Again Mick showed no emotion and remained silent. Sinitsin shook his head in disappointment. "I have never told anybody this fact. I always thought that if you knew, it would mean something to you to discover where you came from."

Mick's voice was deep and threatening. "Would a father let his son be raised by people who only wanted to turn him against his country? Would a father let his son nearly starve in the street before resorting in desperation joining the U.S. Army? Would a father try to threaten his son with death by snipers? Any real father would not let his son be hunted like an animal for years by his colleague and then expect the man to rescue both of them by killing his father's enemy."

Sinitsin's voice cracked as if he were straining with emotion. "I admit that I am not worthy of you. As you say, I am a poor father, but I should tell the whole story to you. We may not get another chance to be together again. I remember the time when Anatoly Baranov and I arrived in East Germany, fresh from training with the KGB, full of vigor and youthful idealism. We were always competitors, Anatoly and I, and we competed for the affections of our superiors as well as the attention of women. We were well-matched for looks and ability and so it went. There was a remarkable beauty working in the Hall of Records at Stasi, and we both went head over heels for her, but she wisely avoided both of us. Both Anatoly and I used every trick to win her over, but Anatoly was given to deceit. He had no scruples, as you people say, and he started using discrete force by getting to her supervisor and her family. Threats from Anatoly can't be dismissed, because he means what he says. I knew him well enough to know that he was considering a rape of this woman if nothing else would work, and I felt compelled to rescue her from him. Of course, I wanted to win her also, but at that time, I wanted her to choose me rather than be forced into it. There, a bit of luck came my way, and just in time. I had secured a small bribe for one of my superiors, who was willing and able to throw a crumb in my direction as a reward. At my suggestion, or perhaps it was begging, he assigned this beautiful specimen of a woman to me as a 'personal assistant.' Anatoly was blind with rage at his misfortune and my good luck and threatened to kill us both. He knew that he couldn't get by with killing me, but this woman we both sought was at risk. Her name, your mother's name, was Greta. Greta Landstrum. I still see her in my dreams, the way the light played in her hair and the smell of her neck. It was easy to fall hopelessly in love with her, and she was all I thought about day and night. At my insistence, we started sharing quarters, because I convinced her that she would be safe from harm there with me. The truth is that she never loved me. Not really. I forced my love into her life, and she tried her best to keep our meager apartment clean and bright, but there was no light in our romance. There was only passion from me and toleration by her. I would have done anything to really make her love me, but it was too late. You can capture a wild bird and put it in a cage, but you know that it is always yearning to be free. The inevitable happened, and she became pregnant...with you. I thought that this would bind us together for life, and I was very happy.

She was morose and looked and acted like an insufferable burden was placed on her. I imagine that she thought that there was always hope of getting away from me until then. For my part, I brought home whatever scant loot that I could acquire to please her but nothing worked, and she remained unhappy. One day I came home, and she was gone. There was no note left, just her absence and a big hollowness inside me. I searched and asked around, but no one knew anything about her. She just vanished. Anatoly feigned sorrow for me, but I could tell that inside he was gloating. I suspected that he was involved but didn't find out the truth for many years." Sinitsin's voice left him for a moment, and he hung his head in silence as the memory of those years flooded back from the yellow past.

After a moment of silence, Mick said, "I know what it's like to love a woman so much that it almost hurts to look at her. My Anna was murdered by your Russian fanatics after only one day...not even twenty-four hours of marriage. I have been in pain since that day, and I know that I can never get past it."

Sinitsin looked up at him. "That is when I discovered your existence, Mick. For a while, you were presumed killed in the explosion. I heard Baranov bragging how he had killed my only son, throwing it in my face. He had arranged the disappearance of Greta by using the Stasi to show up and claim that she was an agent for the West. They carried her to the Berlin Brandenburg gate and threw her across to the Americans. In shame, she gave the baby up, because it was half-Russian. She took up with a caring U.S. soldier and had another baby before Baranov's people murdered her one night. They wanted to cover up any trace of the baby…you…so that Baranov's master plan of planting a young spy in America could never be traced. I swear to you that I never knew anything about any of it until that day. After that moment, I started looking for you right away, but you are a master at hiding. Finally, my young assistant, Sasha, could be sent looking. She is one of the few people I absolutely trust. In my world, loyalty can be bought, and everyone has their price. I can only count a few people in my life that I know will never turn on me. You should also know that I would have been murdered or imprisoned numerous times by now except for my friendship with Putin. He was the KGB officer that I secured a bribe for on several occasions. Even that wouldn't help me if I was found to be plotting against a fellow agent. You have every reason in the world to be the one who gets Baranov. Do it for me and for yourself."

Try as he might to not be deceived by the story laid out by Sinitsin, he felt himself believing it and softening his feeling for this man. It was like a warm breeze came over him, and he relaxed a bit. Occasionally, the small blue dots appeared on Sinitsin's head or chest and then disappeared as quickly.

"There is one more thing that I need to tell you," Sinitsin said. "However, I can show you better than tell you." He switched on a small monitor screen embedded in the back of the seat in front of him. In a moment, there was an infrared video image of a car moving along a familiar street. Without warning another car sped by, abruptly turning in front of the first car, bringing it to a quick stop. Two more cars showed up, one to the side and one in the rear. Two men with automatic weapons ran to the stopped car and pulled the female driver into the street. She clearly was April Chauncy. After she put her hands in the air, one of the men behind her fired a taser into her back, causing her to fall down shaking. They efficiently threw her into the trunk of the lead car and sped away, leaving her car with the driver's door still open. Sinitsin switched off the device and looked at Mick who was becoming more than angry.

"Was that your people who snatched her?" Mick asked him.

"Yes, but before you get violent let me explain that she is unharmed and will be taken to a villa and treated like a queen. It is our way of protecting her. We don't want an international incident which would happen if an FBI agent is involved in the assassination of a Russian national. We don't want to see her hurt or killed either, because we are informed that she is headstrong, and it is the only way to protect her. You have my word that she will be well cared for and released as soon as possible."

"Your word isn't good enough. Where is she?" His voice came up straight from hell, and when he spoke, there was the ominous click of a switchblade opening. The blade that reflected light in his hand was long and tapered. "You will tell me what I want to know right now, or I'll carve off pieces of you and toss them out the window until you do. I don't care if you are my father or not; you will tell me where she is or die a thousand deaths."

Sinitsin obviously never considered that reaction from Mick, and he never expected that the Marines would overpower his own snipers. He had no options. He could die by a bullet or die by knife wound, or he could give Mick what he wanted.

"Mick, you can talk to Sasha. She is trustworthy, and she knows where your FBI associate is." He picked up the car phone and pushed some buttons. The long knife hung in the night air like the demon of death that it was. "Sasha, you need to talk to Mick and reassure him about Agent Chauncy. Yes, I told him that she was to be treated well, but he is threatening to kill me. You must tell him everything." He handed the phone to Mick who took it without words.

"Mick, dearest, is that you?" Sasha said into his ear.

"You have one minute, Sasha, or it ends here," Mick said with a rattle in his voice.

"No, Mick, don't do anything rash. I am right here with her at the Hilton. We brought her in and put her to bed. She is sedated lightly and is unharmed. I promise that she will be well treated, and we only hold her to protect you both. No harm will come to her; I give you my solemn word. I would let you speak to her, but she is asleep just now. Don't worry about her."

Mick spoke while looking directly at Sinitsin. "If anything happens to her or you are lying, there isn't anyplace on earth you can hide from me, and I promise you both a horrible and slow death. I would never stop coming for you. Do you understand this?"

The phone and Sinitsin echoed each other, "Yes, we understand." Mick hung up and sat silently looking at Sinitsin. The blade disappeared with a click.

Mick could see the sweat glistening from Sinitsin's forehead, and they stared at each other in the dark car. The only sound was from the occasional car passing in the street nearby.

"If I do this assassination for you, what happens then?" Mick asked.

"You will rid the world of a menace. I know that you will see less confrontation between our countries and more international cooperation. You will no longer have to hide from my people, and you can return to a life without fear together with our gratitude. If someone doesn't stop him, we are looking at another world war in our future." Sinitsin reached carefully into his pocket under the watchful eye of Mick and pulled out a small folded paper. "Here is the itinerary of Anatoly Baranov. He is scheduled to make various stops on this trip from Moscow, and one of them will be in Berlin. Most frequently, he travels with a large support staff which includes security made of active duty Spetsnaz. They travel by various means and alter plans at the last minute. There are no specific times or places that you can count on them being for certain. They float like a fog from place to place, and Baranov is always preceded by his alert security detail. Killing him will be much harder than killing a U.S. President. If you were lucky enough to get close enough to pull a trigger, you could never escape instant retribution."

"Why is Baranov coming to Berlin?" Mick asked.

"He needs to meet with the local GRU chief to keep him in line. He will go over the latest agenda, probably including you and maybe even me. It is a show of force which reminds everyone whom they actually work for."

Mick thought about it and looked at the paper. "The GRU station chief, who is he?"

Sinitsin chuckled, "His name is Viktor Asmonov, but it will do you no good to know it. He almost never leaves the Russian Embassy, and when he does, it is in a heavily armored car, usually accompanied by a decoy."

"Will Baranov come to the Embassy?" Mick asked.

"Possibly, but more likely he will send for Asmonov, because Baranov can be better protected in a location of his choosing."

Mick said, "It would seem simpler to just use a secure video conference than all the elaborate plans needed in a face-to-face."

Sinitsin shook his woolly head. "No, my son, you should know that the CIA owns the airwaves. There is no secure signal that they can't intercept and break. Besides, there is the intimidation of face-to-face which can't be replaced by anything but the real thing."

"Do not call me your son, and don't think of me as your son, because I am not. As far as I am concerned, you are the enemy of my people and of me, and you should remember that I would kill you for the slightest provocation and without hesitation or emotion."

Alexander Sinitsin sighed at the truth he had just heard. There was no comment possible.

Mick said, "I can use someone on the inside. Can that be Sasha?"

"Absolutely. She is dependable and resourceful. She will do whatever you want. I know that she is attracted to you and looks up to you, and she is loyal to both of us. She is the perfect choice."

"They were hunting her, and she killed one of them. How can she now just walk into the Embassy?" Mick wondered.

"She can't go in as Sasha, of course, but she is, like you, a creature of many cloaks. With the right identification, she is brazen enough to pull it off. She has to be discrete, because some will recognize her, and it has to be a situation of getting in and getting out quickly."

"And, of course, she is expendable," Mick suggested.

"Yes, and that."

Mick thought it over, then said, "You will supply her with identification and clothing to get her inside the Russian Embassy. Looking at this schedule, we have less than one week to get organized. Tell her to contact me in three days when she is ready for a meeting, and together we will get this thing done.

One more thing. If you have harmed even one hair of April Chauncy, you will be the one in my sights."

"Thank you, Mick Grundy, for doing this thing. We will make sure that you are rewarded appropriately, and you will never be sorry," Sinitsin said with sincerity, and he reached out to shake Mick's hand, but his hand remained in the air in vain. Abruptly, Mick opened the car door and walked away. The blue dots again appeared briefly on the face and chest of Sinitsin and then were extinguished.

Mick swung his leg over his bike and pulled on his helmet, waiting for the limousine to depart. Slowly, smoothly, the long black car slipped boat-like out of the lot and moved elegantly into the road. Mick looked around and gave a long thumbs up to whoever was watching. A faraway "OohRah!" came through the trees.

When the bike made the last turn into the underground parking at the U.S. Embassy, Mick could see the uniformed Marine sergeant signaling to him and pointing to a parking spot. When he dismounted, the sergeant asked, "Have a fun time out there tonight, sir?"

"Yes, and thanks to your team, I am still alive to discuss it with you," Mick said as he pulled off the helmet.

"Sir, I am to tell you that Mr. Zeskie is waiting for you in the third floor conference room, and you are to go right up."

"Thank you, Sergeant," Mick said and returned the salute. He hurried for the elevator door which the sergeant held waiting for him.

When Mick approached the room, a staffer was waiting to open the door for him. He was still wearing his leathers and holding his helmet. Present and seated were Ron Zeskie and Elmer Septer, Station Chief of the FBI Berlin. The desk was full of scattered papers, and there were two laptops open. Ron looked up at him with a worried look.

"I don't know how to tell you this," Zeskie began.

"I know that April was snatched tonight. I saw it on a video in Sinitsin's car," Mick said. "His people got her, or so he says. He claims that she is over at the Hilton and is there for her protection. I don't believe anything coming out of them, and we have to find her ourselves and soon."

Zeskie snatched up the phone and barked instructions that the Hilton should be taken apart and April found. When he finished, he said, "Anything else which could help us?"

"Everything is lies. Contact the Germans and see if they know anything. I would have killed Sinitsin tonight when he told me, but I knew if I did, we would lose any hope of getting April back. Right now, I am playing along with them, but I don't want April's kidnapping to be held over my head. The question I have for both of you is how could you let her go out alone like that?" Mick hissed.

Zeskie shook his head. "Mick, she was determined to go out and follow you, uncovering where the mission was taking place from the Marines. Too soon to stop her, she requisitioned a staff car and took off. There was no discussion with anyone about it, and we probably couldn't have prevented her from leaving here, even if we knew."

Elmer Septer asked, "Are you going to carry out an assassination of a Russian National?"

"Did you hear me say that I was?" Mick growled as he leaned toward the face of the FBI chief.

"You didn't say it, but I thought that was what this was all about," Septer said loudly.

"What you don't know, won't hurt you, will it? Right now you should be worrying about your agent and not what I am doing. I don't answer to you on this or anything else, so it's all right that we don't talk to each other again," Mick shouted back.

Elmer Septer rose to his feet glowering. He was not used to disrespect from anyone, and he was very angry.

"Sit down, Elmer. There isn't anyone in this building who can tangle with Mick. Certainly it isn't you. Anyhow, he's right. You have no business asking him anything about an operation out of your jurisdiction. We have enough to worry about," Zeskie said. Elmer dropped into his chair and remained silent.

"What can we do right now, Mick?" Zeskie asked.

"Right now, we make all the contacts we can and continue to hope we can find her, but don't count on accidentally discovering her location. The Russians have squirreled her away somewhere, and until they turn her loose, we aren't going to be able to do much about it. I need to get ready for action, and this is what I need, starting tomorrow. I went to sniper school at Fort Benning, but I need a refresher course, and I want access to a particular fifty caliber piece to train with. Set me up at the *Grafenwoehr* Training Area and get me a XM500. I will leave for there before dawn. Supply false credentials stating that I am in the German Army, and I need a personal instructor to work with me and me only. You may need to get hold of General Adams to make this work. Another thing. I want to take the rifle with me when I leave, and I want an assortment of explosive ordnance for it and a fitted backpack to carry it all in."

Zeskie mulled it over. "You and your brother are about the same size. His rank as *Oberst* would do it. Think you can borrow an outfit from him?"

"I'll call him tonight, but I'm sure he will do anything in his power for me."

"You take care of the uniform and getting down there. By the time you arrive, they will be waiting for you. Good shooting," Zeskie said.

Chapter 19

The Big Gun

Grafenwoehr, Southern Germany
0630 Hours

He had departed at 0300 hours from Berlin, and in the dawn light, he could make out the guard post of the *Grafenwöhr* south entrance. He was stiff from riding, and the air was chilly, making the gravel crunch under the hard tires. He pulled up to the barricade, looked around and unzipped his leather jacket, which was over his brother's black jumpsuit. He was reaching for his credentials just as one of the four MPs close by came up to him.

"You will remove your helmet," the soldier barked. Mick quickly complied and then offered his papers. The sergeant took the papers from him and said, "You will shut down your machine and step this way." Mick obediently complied. He left his helmet on the rearview mirror and walked toward the guard shack. In the near distance, he could see the muzzle and turret of an Abrams tank, and a platoon of regular U.S. Army standing in loose formation near the tank. Some of them were looking his way. The sergeant disappeared inside and left him standing alone. After a short time, the door opened, and the sergeant came to a stiff salute.

"*Oberst* Brauer, they are expecting you. You will please park your motorcycle in that area on your left and wait beside it until your instructor arrives. Take all your belongings with you. On behalf of the U.S. Army, welcome to *Grafenwoehr*, and we hope that your training is helpful."

In German-accented English, Mick said, "Thank you, Sergeant, it will be most helpful," and returned the salute with clicked heels. Before Mick finished parking the bike, he could see a light brown Humvee rapidly approaching him.

The machine skidded to a stop, and the driver shouted through the door. "If you be Brauer, get in." Mick opened the door and grinned at the master sergeant and swung in. The Humvee lurched forward with a jerk, and the driver extended his hand for a shake. "My name is Charles Willford Howard, Master Sergeant U.S. Army. You can call me Shotgun, like everybody else does. I am the chief instructor with the fifty caliber sniper school. I am yours for the day, as ordered, and we are headed right to the range. Is that acceptable?"

Mick attempted to answer over the roar of the Humvee's motor and the wind noise but only managed to nod yes. He took a long look at his driver as they banged down the dirt road. He was around 40, but wiry and hard-looking, with leathered face and arms. He had a Green Beret hat cocked to one side and a large tattoo on his forearm which said, "Army." They eventually arrived at a small barracks, and the crack of rifle fire could be heard just over the rise.

"Usually, the first step is to learn to break down and assemble the equipment, *Oberst.* I have to ask if you have any previous experience in sniper training."

"Yes, Shotgun, I have." Shotgun looked at him pensively but didn't comment.

"Say, Shotgun, I came in from Berlin this morning without breakfast. Got any food handy?"

"Sure I do. I always keep some rations in my bag. C or K?" Shotgun asked, offering one of each. Mick reached for the C ration and sat down to eat. Shotgun passed him a bottle of water and asked, "Say, if I can ask, what do you intend to do with this sniper training?"

Mick looked back at him and said, "Why, Shotgun, I intend to kill with it." They laughed at the obvious answer. When Mick was finished with his ration, they started in earnest taking the weapon apart and putting it back together.

"Sir, only a couple of things you gotta know. The rifle comes apart in only three pieces. There is the upper receiver assembly and the lower receiver assembly and the bolt. Never take the scope off of the rifle or you will have to sight it in again, and I assume that you want it to fire right on the first shot. This rifle can be made to fit in a package as short as 34 inches, disassembled. Together with two clips of ten rounds, it weighs thirty-two pounds. A heavy weapon to carry a long way. Clumsy also. There are lighter sniper rifles, are you sure that you need this one?" Shotgun asked.

"There may be a need to stop a car and to penetrate some light armor," Mick answered.

Shotgun nodded. "This is your baby, then. There is a silencer made for this weapon. Illegal by international treaty, but we still have them. It really works but reduces the range and accuracy of the weapon. Interested?"

"No, noise won't matter. I'll be too far away."

"Another question, sir. There are at least twenty different types of ordnance for this weapon. They all sight in a little differently so we want to practice with what you are going to use. What will it be?"

"Do you have any of the Mk 211 Mod 0 HEIAP available?" Mick asked.

"Yes, sir. Now I see where this is going. We are going to have to go to another training area for that round, because there is too much danger for our pit spotters. If you will wait here, sir, I will have some ammo brought over, and we can go shooting."

True to his word, Shotgun had an ammo box quickly delivered by Humvee, and they piled into it for a short trip to the tank training area. Shotgun went out and set up some targets, and together they set up the shooting station on a small hill. He fastened a small telescope on a tripod and focused on the closer target.

"The first target is at 300 yards, the second is at 600 and so forth. If we want, we can fire at some really long range targets at 2000 yards. Long enough, *Oberst?*" Mick nodded and smiled at him then spread out on the sand, taking his time with the first shot.

"Crack."

"Dead on target, sir. Go ahead and try the 600. Adjust for distance on the scope," Shotgun said as he peered through the long range scope.

"Crack."

"Got it again. Nice shooting. Move to the next one. I'm detecting a small crosswind of five knots," Shotgun said.

"Crack."

"Perfect," Shotgun stopped and looked Mick over carefully. Something was bothering him.

"Shotgun? You have a question?" Mick asked.

"Look, sir, there are only the two of us out here. I've been at this a long time, and I can say for sure that you were trained by our Special Forces. You are no German, are you?"

"It's just between the two of us, Shotgun. You are right, but forget that you know it. As far as you know, I am just some German officer that you trained on request. You don't want to know more than that."

"Thanks for leveling with me, sir. I understand that you are tuning up for a mission and that the U.S. Army isn't party to it, at least officially. I got it."

"Want to try the 2000 yard one, Shotgun?" Mick asked.

"Well, sir, if you can hit that one two out of three shots, you are as good as I have seen. Let me check out the winds first." Shotgun studied the target for a long time before speaking. "Variable winds up to 10 knots. Hard, hard shot, sir. See what you can do with it."

"Crack."

"Crack."

"Crack."

On the last round, there was a fireball seen at the target area, the target disappearing as a spiraling column of smoke rose into the blue sky. Mick looked up at Shotgun who was laughing. "Well, sir, I was watching. The first two hit the target and the third hit the wooden support. You can see the effect of the incendiary bullet. It will take out anything, including most tanks. Takes more that four inches of armor steel to stop one of these bullets. Far as I am concerned, you are as good as snipers get. Congratulations."

"Thanks, Shotgun. I enjoyed it a lot. Got time for a beer somewhere?" Mick asked.

"Well, I have a better idea. Let me come with you on your mission. I'll bet you need a spotter as well as backup, and I would love to be with you." He slapped Mick on the shoulder with some affection.

"Shotgun, I'd go to hell and back with you. I'm very complimented that you feel that way, because I feel the same about you. This isn't that kind of enemy. This is spy work and an upright guy like you would be visible for fifty miles or more. I have to do the job alone, but there is one more thing you can do for me."

"Name it, sir, and it's yours," Shotgun said.

"You saw that I rode in here on a sport bike. I need a rig to carry this rifle on the bike without attracting a lot of attention. Got any ideas?"

"No, but I know people who can help. Come with me." They gathered their gear and got in the Humvee.

After a few minutes of dirt roads, they came to an area of Quonset structures, and Shotgun pulled up and got out. He came back to the Humvee with a couple of large men in coveralls.

"Here is what we want to do. Take this rifle and ammo and attach it to a sport bike without interfering with the rider and without making it obvious what he is carrying. Can you do it?" Shotgun asked them.

Jake, the older of the two, said, "Go bring the motorcycle over here, and by the time you get here, we will have figured it out." Mick and Shotgun did just that, and an hour later he was outfitted and ready to ride. The gun was in a black case and positioned like a diagonal saddle bag just to the right rear of the rider. Because of the black color, it was not obviously anything other than a slightly awkward saddle bag. Mick shook hands with all of them and pulled Shotgun over to one side.

"My friend, I have to say goodbye, but you have helped me a lot today, and I wish we could spend more time together. Someday, perhaps, I will be back for another favor."

"Well, *Oberst*," he said smiling, "some people are always welcome. If you change your mind, I am willing to help you, and I might be the only person who can shoot as well as you can. Remember that."

It was nearly 0300 hours when he arrived back at the American Embassy in Berlin. He rolled in and was saluted by the Marine on duty. He left the bike with the gun still attached and crept up to the sleeping area and dropped on the bed. Before he drifted off to sleep, the door opened, and Zeskie came in.

"Hey, did it go well for you today, Mick?"

"Yes, thanks for setting it up, Zeskie. Any word about locating April?"

"No. Nobody saw anything or knows anything. We have no leads," Zeskie admitted. "What are your plans now?"

"I need to spend the next twenty-four hours figuring out a plan. You need to brainstorm with me and develop something. Other than that, we are waiting on Sasha to contact me. Tonight, what remains of it, I need to sleep."

Zeskie got the message. "See you later then. Sleep well," and he left.

Chapter 20

The Plan

1100 hours

Zeskie was sipping his coffee when Mick staggered in. He looked tired and rubbed his face in his hands in an attempt to wake up. "Long day yesterday, Mick," Zeskie observed.

"What can you tell me, Zeskie?"

"Nothing, I'm afraid. Just like you thought, April was not at the Hilton. We and the Germans searched every room. She was never there. We have no leads." Zeskie watched him over the steam in his cup.

"They have pulled out all stops to get me to do this for them. Lies, threats and now kidnapping of my partner. There is nothing left for them to try," Mick said.

"Are you going to do it?"

"Yeah, I am. It's just another Russian to pop as far as I'm concerned. What can I lose?"

"Probably your life, that's all," Zeskie observed.

"My life!" Mick laughed. "It hasn't been worth much lately. Death would at least be a relief for me."

"For a walking dead man, you sure have a lot of people who care about you. Look around. April, for instance, walked right into hell for you. Went out not knowing where she was going or what she was going to do when she got there. She doesn't even speak German. And it was all for you...for you, Mick."

"Yes, I know that she did. It was what a true partner should do, but she put us both at risk and reduced my options."

Zeskie said, "On to the plan. Any ideas?"

"One more thing I need. I am going to get Sasha to entrap one of the drivers for the GRU station chief and plant a bug on him. The bug needs to be silent until activated, otherwise they may find it during an electronic sweep. From what Sinitsin said, they use two cars to transport him, one is a decoy. We need to determine which one he actually uses and who drives it. When he leaves, we will track him straight to Baranov."

Zeskie thought about it and said, "If she gets a look in the cars, the one Viktor Asmonov uses will have a vodka bar in the back. We have a tracking device which looks just like a typical credit card. It can be triggered by satellite when we want it to send a signal, but first Sasha has to get it into his wallet. As I see it, even if you can track Asmonov to his meeting with Baranov, you still might not get a clear shot, assuming that you can get close enough."

"It's the best we can do," Mick said. "About finding April...I have an idea I plan to try out this afternoon which may generate a lead."

"What is it," Zeskie said with worry.

"Simple, I'll be the bait that catches the fish which pursues me."

Mick took the rifle kit off the motorcycle, entrusting it to one of the nearby Marines, and checked his pistol one last time. After powering up the Embassy's underground ramp toward the street, his motorcycle moved through traffic aggressively but not so rapidly that a determined tail couldn't keep up. Watching his rearview mirrors, he kept seeing flashes of light reflected from a small white car. He rode around as if he was intent on a destination but was careful not to let his tail fall too far behind. The white car was always there, sometimes a block away, at times only two cars back. Mick led the way to the outskirts of Berlin where older, larger buildings were spaced farther apart, and the traffic diminished. A block behind him, the white car just completed its turn when Mick abruptly accelerated, turning three corners rapidly. After completing the last turn, he could see the white car pausing at an intersection, looking for him. He accelerated hard then braked to stop alongside the car, silently pointing his 45 through the open passenger window. The driver was caught by surprise and looked around anxiously, as if expecting help to appear out of thin air.

"Поместите ваши руки в прямом эфире и выйдите из автомобиля," ["Put your hands in the air and get out of the car,"] The man looked intently at the street ahead as if considering another option. Mick pulled the hammer back with a click. The driver started shaking and put his arms in the air. Mick waited, and the gun remained pointed at the man's face. Slowly he got out of the car and stood at the curb,

hands in the air. Mick walked to the trunk and waved the man to come to him. The man complied slowly, knowing what was about to happen. Mick's gun came down on the man's forehead with a *waap*, and the man fell unconscious to the street.

Andrei Nikolaevich came into consciousness slowly. Terrifying pain radiated from his shoulders, and he found that he couldn't move his arms. His head dangled toward his feet, and he could see that there was dirt beneath him. Thin rays of sunlight streamed through broken boards as slots of light, lighting up the dusty room in a hazy glow. A large rough hand came into his view, and Andrie's head snapped back and up. Andrie realized that he was nearly suspended in air, his arms behind him. His shoulders were killing him, and he groaned from the pain.

"Теперь мы готовы иметь нашу беседу, Андрея," ["Now we are ready to have our conversation, Andrei,"] the voice said. It was deep and frightening like in some nightmare he had as a child.

"English, I speak English, Grundy," Andrei sputtered.

"Good. English. Now is when I should tell you that you have a choice to defect or die. I want to save a lot of time today, so I need to demonstrate to you your third choice," the voice said. There was a click, and in a split second a piercing intense pain exploded from Andrei's leg. He looked down to see a long knife blade going through his thigh from outside to in. "Now if I turn the blade a little and pull up, there will be a huge wound in your leg."

"No! No! Stop. Please, I will talk," Andrei screamed.

"Oh, not yet, Andrei. Please, some resistance first. We need to be sure that you know what to be afraid of, don't we?" the voice said. There was a flash, and the blade stabbed into his cheek, passing out the other side of his face, just above his tongue. He could taste blood and feel the sharp blade with his tongue and teeth. He gurgled on what seemed to be a river of blood spilling down his throat. "Now, if I turn the blade a bit and pull, your mouth will extend from ear to ear. Very attractive. Want to try?" There was loud gurgling and an extended groan. Mick pulled the blade out, allowing Andrei's head to hang down, a steady stream of blood and saliva pooling on his feet. "Andrei, there are only the two of us in here, and there is no one coming to save you. You have to make me happy, or you have only had a small sample of what is coming."

"Anything, Grundy. I tell you anything. Please no more," Andrei sputtered.

"I want to know where you took April Chauncy, the FBI Agent. Don't dare deny that you weren't involved, because I saw the same car that you drove today on the video. You were there when she was taken."

"Yes, but the other agents took her. I don't know where she is." Andrei said plaintively.

"That's too bad for you, Andrei. Have you ever heard of a woman getting a mastectomy for breast cancer? They cut off the breast to cure it. I'm going to do the same operation for you right now to cure you of lying." Mick took the sharp switchblade and opened Andrei's shirt, exposing his chest. He drew a circle around the pectoralis muscle with the tip of the blade, causing a thin line of blood to follow the knife around the chest. "You know the best part of this? You have two breasts so we can practice and get it right. You should be warned that this will be a bit bloody."

"Okay, Grundy," he gurgled. Mick played with the tip of the knife on Andrei's chest while he waited for him to tell what he knew. "They will kill me for this. I don't know exactly where the safe house is, but I know the neighborhood. You should be able to find it yourself. Go to the corner of *Darwinstrasse* and *Quedlinburger Strasse*. There is a kinky sex place there. The place you seek is close by, but I have never actually seen it myself. She will be heavily guarded."

"Andrei, if I go to this place and come back empty handed...you know what will happen to you?"

"Yes, the same thing which will happen if I go back. They will know that I talked. I am doomed." He started to sob, hanging from his hands and drooling blood.

"There is a chance for you after all, Andrei. But only one choice remains...defect to our side. You have nothing to lose. Do you agree, Andrei Nikolaevich? Andrei nodded his head causing more blood and saliva to pour out of his mouth and cheeks. "Tell you what, Andrei, if you are right about this location, I'll send someone out to rescue you and repair your injuries. If you have lied to me, I'll be the one who returns. Hang around and find out what will happen."

Mick returned to his motorcycle, still parked by the curb as he had left it. Throwing the keys to the white car into the sewer, he started the bike, heading for the address unwillingly supplied by Andrei. At first, he slowly rode by looking the area over. A small shop advertising sex stood near the intersection with buildings behind and beside it, any of them suitable locations for a safe house. He parked in the small gravel lot and entered the small dark shop, standing in the doorway for a moment, letting his eyes adjust to the dim light. Scattered couples mingled on tattered couches to the smell of hashish hanging in the air. A small buxom girl with stiff platinum blond hair came smiling up to him and put her hand on his arm.

"Meine, was für ein schöner Mann. Du siehst einsam, schöner Mann. Was kann ich für Sie tun heute Abend." ["My, what a handsome man. You look lonely, handsome man. What can I do for you tonight?"]

Mick smiled at her and touched her hair *"Ich brauche ein paar Informationen, und ich werde auch für sie eine solche charmante und schöne junge Dame zu bezahlen."* ["I need some information, and I will pay well for it to such a charming and beautiful young lady."]

The girl frowned at this unusual request, pulling away from him. *"Sind Sie von der Polizei?"* ["Are you from the police?"]

"Nein. Es geht um eine Spielschulden. In letzter Zeit gesehen keine Russen hier?" ["No. This is about a gambling debt. Seen any Russians around here

lately?]

The girl put her finger to her lips and said, *"Es wird Sie fünfzig Euro kosten."* ["It will cost you fifty euros."]

"Ich werde Ihnen einhundert Euro geben, aber ich will die Information zuerst." ["I'll give you one hundred euros, but I want the information first."]

"Es gibt vier verschiedene, die ich gesehen hier sind gekommen. Sie sind beängstigend. Aber ich erinnere mich nicht sehen, jede für mehrere Tage..." ["There are four different ones that I have seen come in here. They are scary. But, I don't remember seeing any for several days."]

Mick took a wad of euros from his pocket and gave her a hundred. He wrote a number down for her and handed her both. *"Rufen Sie mich an, wenn sie zurückkommen, und ich gebe Ihnen eine weitere hundert."* ["Call me if they come back and I'll give you another hundred."]

He walked outside and looked around carefully. There were no clues apparent, no strange cars or men standing guard. Two vacant looking buildings toward the rear looked interesting so he walked toward them being alert for any movement. His phone rang.

"Mick, this is Ron Zeskie. Sasha was just admitted to a local hospital. She has been beaten and has some injuries. She is at *CBF Hindenburgdamm.* We were alerted by the BND, and Peter Koffman is over there right now. She has been asking to see you. Think you could swing by and see her before you come back in?"

"Sure will, Zeskie. I'll get right over there. There is a possibility that the Russians are using a safe house to hold April. I'm at the location given by one I captured today, but we need a couple of search teams to come down here and go through all these buildings."

"We'll get the Germans to do it right away."

"By the way, I left the one I interviewed hanging in a barn. Your guys should pick him up and get him some medical care." He gave Zeskie the location and hung up. He went back to his motorcycle and headed out to the hospital.

Charité – Universitätsmedizin Berlin: Campus Benjamin Franklin (CBF)

The hospital complex was huge, modern and spotlessly clean. Mick felt strange and out of place walking in the front doors dressed in his black leathers. As soon as he entered the lobby, he was greeted by a policeman who must have been waiting for him to arrive.

"Mick Grundy?" the policeman asked politely. Mick nodded yes, and the man indicated he was to follow, leading the way down a maze of corridors, two different elevator systems and finally shown into a holding area where the beds were separated by curtains on overhead tracks. The broad shoulders of his brother, Peter, bent over the hospital bed. Mick came up behind him and placed his hand on his brother's shoulder. Sasha was lying down, her pain made obvious by her furrowed brow and puckered lips. A young physician was in attendance on the other side of the bed.

"Кто сделал это к Вам, Sasha?" ["Who did this to you, Sasha?"] Mick asked.

"Мои собственные люди сделали это, когда я пожаловался о лгании Вам. Они хотели удостовериться, что я знал, кто был ответственным. Кроме того, Sinitsin обижается на мою привлекательность к Вам." ["My own people did it when I complained about lying to you. They wanted to make sure I knew who was in charge. Also, Sinitsin resents my attraction to you."]

Mick acknowledged the young physician, asking, *"Was sind ihre Verletzungen?"* ["What are her injuries?"]

The doctor looked toward *Oberst* Koffman for permission to answer. Peter consented, adding, "You may answer in English, Doctor."

"She only has scant bruises that you can actually see. They were skilled in hitting her where it doesn't show. She has two fractured ribs from a kick, and we are watching her for internal injuries and bleeding. There is blood in the urine which may indicate renal injury, but it may be tomorrow before I can tell you more," the doctor said in perfect English.

Mick looked at Peter and asked, "Where did you pick her up?"

"A local policeman witnessed her being thrown from a moving car about four blocks from the American Embassy. He had her taken here. The BND intercepted the call and here I am."

"Sasha, I don't understand. If your people wanted you to help me, why would they nearly kill you before we could get together? I instructed Sinitsin that you were to be given clothes and ID and then you were to contact me."

"They did all that, and I am still expected to help you. I am being taught to follow instructions without complaint. This is nothing new for me. It has happened before and worse," Sasha said with a clear and level voice.

Mick waited in silence as the physician finished the taping of her rib fractures and departed. Leaning close to his brother's ear he said, "Could you wait outside in the hall until I talk with her in private?" Peter nodded and quickly left Mick and Sasha alone.

"I discovered your lie about having April in the Hilton, and I am very angry about it."

"Of course I lied. I was expected to lie. We were listening to the conversation and knew what Sinitsin said. I had to back him up, or you would have killed him right there, wouldn't you?"

"Possibly, or at least cut him up a bit," Mick admitted. "So, it's clear that April is being held hostage to insure that I will do what Sinitsin wants. Will they harm her?"

"I don't know who has her or where she is. They don't trust me that far. I don't know what the plans are for her now or later, but she is a tool like me...use us and throw us away."

"You could have defected, Sasha. You would be safe right now. I would have made sure you were."

"You need me, Mick Grundy. You can't do this without me so I am here for you alone, there is no other reason. I no longer believe in any cause, and when this is over, I will go with you anywhere you wish." She laid her hand gently on the back of his arm, her tears flowing down her cheeks. Even in hospital garments, her hair matted, and her lips swollen, she was incredibly gorgeous. Mick had to briefly look away from her face to regain his composure.

He reached out and touched the side of her face. "I'll come and see you in the morning. Stay here until I arrive, understood?"

"Yes, Mick. Tomorrow I will be well enough to discuss plans with you. The time for us to act is near."

Mick winked at her and turned to leave. He found Peter in the hall and pulled him away from the door so that Sasha couldn't overhear the conversation.

"Peter, can you get a guard posted for her tonight? I don't want her to be harmed any more, and I don't want her to leave here without me."

"Of course, Mick. We already have some people on the way. Did you find anything new about April?"

"I have a possible lead regarding her location. Zeskie is supposed to contact you and organize a search in a certain area. That's all we have so far."

"Mick, just what is going on. Can you tell me?"

"No, Peter. Trust me, you don't want to be involved. You heard your Director disclaim any assistance, just as the American government has done. This is something I am doing alone, so that only I will get the blame. If I succeed, you will certainly hear about it, and I may need some help getting away from here, but for now, I just want your help to find April."

"I'll take personal charge of any search. At the first sign of her, we will call you, I promise," Peter said and patted Mick on his shoulder.

236

Chapter 21

Trusting Sasha

Charité - Universitätsmedizin Berlin
0830 hours

Mick nodded at the German uniformed policeman as he turned the corner toward Sasha's room. They had moved her during the night to a private room, and just before Mick found the room, he noticed the young physician who had been with Sasha the previous day.

"Excuse me, Doctor, may I ask you a question?" Mick asked.

"Certainly, I remember you from yesterday. This is about the young girl in 453, I assume?"

"Yes, Doctor. Is she able to be discharged today?" Mick asked politely.

"I would recommend another two days of observation. Should she have a splenic injury, we may not see the signs yet, and there is the troubling and continuing blood in her urine."

"Has she been up on her feet yet?"

"Only to the toilet. She is very sore this morning."

Mick thanked him and continued to the room. Sasha was sitting up and unsuccessfully trying to comb her hair with a hospital supplied plastic comb. She smiled at Mick when she saw him and put down the comb. Without saying anything, Mick picked up the comb and started working on her long hair.

"How are you feeling this morning?" he asked.

"Oh, I feel normal today. We have to get back to work, so you can tell them to discharge me," she said.

"That is not what your physician just told me, Sasha. You are plenty banged up, and you can't even lift your arms to comb your own hair."

"Do you find me attractive this morning, Mick?"

"I would compare you to a ripe peach hanging from a tree. So tempting."

"Ooo, I like that! Can you help me put on my things so we can leave?" She looked up at him in anticipation, her big eyes fluttering appealingly.

He knew that she had to leave. Today was the last day of preparation, and according to the schedule, Baranov was due in Berlin in forty-eight hours. Mick needed her help to plant the bug on the driver. There was no choice, and they both knew it. He opened her locker and took the plastic bag of clothes and opened it on the bed. When he looked up, he realized that she had stood up beside the bed and had dropped her hospital garment on the floor. Well, at one time, he thought he would like to see her unclothed, and now he was going to get an eyeful. She was standing there naked, waiting on him to assist her in putting on her clothing, silently watching him for any reaction. Her body compelled him to look at her, and he was taken aback by her physical beauty. She was like the best of any sculpture, perfect in form, flawless in color, her long brown hair hanging off of her shoulder, partially covering one perfect breast.

"Bra first, Mick," she suggested, extending her slender arms. Mick silently went about dressing her, one article at a time. She would occasionally catch her breath from rib pain as she moved or inhaled. The panties were next. Such perfect buttocks he noted. He resisted the urge to touch her unnecessarily. When he knelt down, she lifted her foot, and he slipped on her shoes, one at a time. Her dress was soiled and torn from tumbling onto the street, and he could see an area of abrasion on her thigh through one of the rents.

"Your clothing is in tatters," he observed.

"If you will take me to the train station, there should be a new outfit waiting there in a locker. The identification we need will also be there."

"Is that all then?" he asked, and looked around the room.

"It is all I have. Can you give me your arm for the trip out of the hospital?

They walked out of the room, arm in arm like lovers. Mick stopped to talk to the policeman and told him that he was taking responsibility for her now and thanked him for his protection last night. The officer was glad to get away from standing in the hall and happily waved goodbye to both of them. They made their way slowly and painfully out into the morning sunlight and the parking lot. Sasha took a deep breath and was caught by the intense pain from her ribs.

"Oops, I'm not yet ready for that," she said, attempting a weak smile.

They drove across town in a car supplied by Peter, toward the train station and Sasha's locker. During the trip, Mick started discussing his plan with her. "Sasha, I think that if we can figure out which limo the GRU station chief uses, you can slip a tracking device into his driver's wallet, allowing us to track the car to the rendezvous with Baranov."

Sasha looked surprised "You mean the driver for Viktor Asmonov?"

"Yes, do you know him?"

"Yes, his name is Dmitri, but he goes by Danny. He is a fat slob and has been trying to seduce me since I first came to Germany."

"You mean that you know that this Danny is for sure the driver for Asmonov?"

"Yes, Danny brags that he is the only driver Asmonov will trust."

Mick thought about this fortunate link for a moment. "Does this Danny know that Baranov's people are hunting you?"

"He probably does. That will be even better, because I might convince him to help me hide. Of course, he will expect to be paid in sex. He would crawl over hot coals to get his hands on my body," she laughed and then held her side with her hand.

"You are in no condition to have sex with a fat man, Sasha," Mick said with some concern.

"You wouldn't have any jealousy about it, would you, Mick?"

"Some," he admitted.

"No, that is my out. I am too sore for sex. He will have to put me somewhere to recover for a while. Probably he will suggest an apartment."

"Does he have an apartment?" Mick wondered.

"I don't think that they would let him live away from the car. He probably sleeps in the basement, right beside it," she giggled. "I will insist that he find an apartment for me. I am sure he will do it."

Sasha waited in the car when Mick went into the train station to collect the package left in her locker. He approached the locker with caution and stood back from the door when it opened. There seemed to be no one interested in him or his actions, and he returned to the car with the package under his arm and threw it on the seat. Before they left, Sasha opened the package, expressing surprise at the stylish clothing it contained. There were two separate identity cards using different names, both with her photograph. She pick up a small telephone, studying it closely, when Mick snatched it away and tossed it out the window.

"Go over every inch of that stuff and look for bugs," he demanded. "I can't take you back to the American Embassy, because your people are sure to be watching that building carefully. We are going to get a hotel room to use as a base of operations. You could lure Danny there."

"Yes, try to find one close to the Russian Embassy."

"What about the Grand Westin? It is only three blocks from your Embassy?" Mick asked.

"I have seen it, but it was always too fine for any of

us to go in. How can you afford this?" she asked.

"Not for you to worry about. We'll head over there and get established. They would never think to look there for us. You have to change these raggy clothes first, or it will raise eyebrows in the lobby."

"Find a public restroom and come in with me to help me on with my clothes," she suggested.

"Coffee cafe all right?" he asked as he turned hard into a parking place. They took the bundle of clothes and went in and found a table. Mick ordered two coffees, while watching the ladies' room carefully. When at last it was free, they went in together. To help Sasha out of her dress, Mick carefully slit the sides with his knife, and the dress fell away. Painfully, they got the new clothing over her arms, and when she was dressed, Mick appraised her.

"You look as attractive as ever and your injuries don't show. Do you think that you are able to walk in there and pull this off?" he asked tenderly.

"I have to try, don't I? Do you have the tracking device to plant on him?"

Mick found the card in his pocket. It looked well-used and appeared like any other credit card. "Here it is. Don't worry about them finding it, because until activated, it is undetectable."

"How does it work?" she asked.

"We have to keep watch on the Russian Embassy. When Asmonov's car leaves the building, we transmit a signal by satellite which turns on the card. The card will emit an impulse at five second intervals for nearly twelve hours. I have a small laptop which does the tracking. That means we have to follow and get in position quickly, because when the car stops, we will have little time to act.”

“If you manage to shoot at Baranov, they will find you and kill you. He will have two other cars with him, full of experienced and highly trained men.”

“It won’t matter if I am far enough away.”

“You know that they will figure out who did this, and they eventually will find the tracking device. They will be hunting both of us,” Sasha said.

“Didn’t you hear Sinitsin say that he will come to power if Baranov is taken out and that all will be forgiven? I am also counting on him to release April as he promised.” Sasha was silent and just looked at him with a blank expression. Someone started pounding on the restroom door, and they were forced to leave.

They stopped at the small shop in the Westin ground floor to purchase Sasha’s cosmetics. She moved slowly and stiffly. They stopped for snacks and drinks before finding the room. Once in, they sat across from each other at the small table.

“Are you ready to try this?” he asked.

“I think I should go over there now and just walk into the parking area and let Danny find me. Because there are too many things which can happen to foil our plan, I will have to act on opportunity,” Sasha said.

“You will have to get him alone to place the card,” Mick observed.

“And drunk on vodka.”

“Not much of a plan,” Mick said. She shrugged. There was a lot riding on her success with this fellow

Danny, but she seemed confidant that the man's attraction to her would be strong enough for him to let down his guard. Mick knew that the female trap was always a good one, and better men that this fat driver have fallen into it. He turned on the small computer to test the link, and he was able to turn on and off the tracking card just by a click of the mouse. But all of it depended on a fat man's urges and a bit of luck. After talking, they decided that Sasha was to walk the three blocks to the Russian Embassy by herself starting at 1600 hours. They had time for a short rest, and they lay on the big bed together, looking at the ceiling.

"Want to have sex with me to relax you?" Sasha asked, without looking at him.

"Of course I do. But we are not doing that now. Too many complications. There is time for that if we get through what is coming. Besides, you are too sore for that sort of thing," Mick answered.

She extended her arm and let her hand fall on his privates. She gave a couple of squeezes. "I think your body knows more than you, Mick." He gently removed her hand and patted her arm.

"Behave yourself, Sasha. I am trying to think our plan through. Our lives depend on getting this right."

The short afternoon went by quickly, and Mick rolled to his feet and gently pulled Sasha to hers. "Get ready, dear, it's time."

Russian Embassy Parking Garage
1601 hours

Dmitri was bending over the fender of the dark red

limousine, polishing the paint, when he noticed a female silhouette coming toward him, its hips swaying seductively. He stood erect for a good look, but the light was behind her, and all that he could tell was that she was shapely and had long hair. As she got closer, she said, *"Здравствуйте, Дэнни. Действительно ли Вы счастливы видеть меня?"* ["Hello, Danny. Are you happy to see me?"]

"Sasha! Они ищут Вас. Почему - Вы здесь?" ["Sasha! They are looking for you. Why are you here?"]

She came up close to him and touched him on the arm. *"Они рассердились на меня вчера и травмировали меня и бросили меня от автомобиля как часть хлама. Я только вышел из больницы. Мои ребра сломаны, и я нигде не должен пойти. Я нуждаюсь в некоторой помощи."* ["They got mad at me yesterday and hurt me and threw me from the car like a piece of trash. I just got out of the hospital. My ribs are broken, and I have nowhere to go. I need some help."]

She stood there in front of him, the tears streaming down her beautiful face. Such a picture would soften any man, and Dmitri was not any man. He was a man who was already enthralled by the lovely Sasha. He dreamed about her constantly, and here she was in his hands.

"Это было бы опасным для меня помочь Вам." ["It would be dangerous for me to help you."]

"Я не сделал что-нибудь неправильно. Они не имеют никакой причины преследовать меня, потому что я - лояльный русский. Я не знаю, где еще повернуться, Дэнни." ["I haven't done anything wrong. They have no reason to pursue me, because I am a loyal Russian. I

don't know where else to turn, Danny."]

Dmitri couldn't resist putting his arm around her waist, but when he did she recoiled in pain. She pulled her blouse open enough to show him the tape over her ribs.

Dmitri looked around the garage and saw that they were alone. *"Как Вы заканчивали охранники?"* ["How did you get past the guards?"] Sasha reached into her purse and pulled out an identification with her photograph but using another name. She handed it to Dmitri.

After he looked it over carefully he said, *"Это превосходно. Они не знают, что Вы - здесь."* ["This is excellent. They do not know that you are here."]

"Вы поможете мне, тогда?" ["Will you help me then?"]

Dmitri's eyes were wild, and he put his hand to his mouth in thought. *"Я имею представление. Вы будете ждать прямо здесь. Не уезжайте, пока я не возвращаюсь."*["I have an idea. You will wait right here. Do not leave until I return."] He left abruptly, discarding his polishing rag on the concrete floor. Sasha watched as he ambled off like a crazed Russian bear, leaving her alone beside the red limousine that was the object of her mission. She looked around carefully before trying the driver's door, finding it unlocked. She slowly and quietly pulled it fully open and quickly looked inside, detecting a small pocket beside the seat where the carpet was not fully fastened. The credit card tracking device slid deeply into the cleft and then she quietly closed the door, innocently strolling away up the ramp, past the guards, and onto the street. Her part of the mission had been accomplished.

A few minutes later, Dmitri drove up in a little battered French car belonging to a coworker. He had given the man a 500 ruble note for use of the car and was beaming with anticipation. Regretfully, Sasha was already gone.

On her way back to the Westin, Sasha took the long route, using her skills in tradecraft to advantage. As she passed a trash can, she dropped the identity card inside. It was of no further use, because they would be looking for her under that name. When she got back to the room, she found a note from Mick.

"Left for some supplies and to see how the search for April is going. Back soon. Order some food to be sent up, and I will be right back."

Chapter 22

On The Move

American Embassy
2200 hours

Mick found Zeskie in his office and entered without knocking.

"Mick! How is your planning proceeding?" Zeskie asked, smiling.

"Listen, Zeskie, I know that you always know what is going on. I am never sure how or where all that information comes from, but I know I don't need to tell you anything."

"Then what can I do for you?"

"I know that you people keep a careful eye on the Russians. You are only a couple of blocks away. Do you have an ongoing video feed from their parking area?"

Zeskie hesitated. "Yes, Mick, in fact there are several."

"I need to tap into one of them to know when that car of Viktor Asmonov leaves, so I can turn on the tracking device," Mick said.

"Okay. I'll give you the password to tap into one of them if that will help. Has Sasha planted the device on the driver?"

"She is working on it now," Mick answered.

"I hear that she was badly treated, even in the hospital until this morning. How is she handling it?"

"She is as tough as any man. Just better looking. What about April?"

"We are cooperating with the Germans, and right now there are two teams examining the area you suggested and we are going to go door to door, but so far nothing. The Russian that you cut up has been rescued. He is being held by the Germans, and we are trying to determine if he is worth keeping. He talked a lot but most of what he told us, we already knew by other sources. What is next for you?"

"I think tomorrow will see some action, and I am as ready as I can be given the unknowns," Mick said.

"This Sasha. Can you trust her with your life?"

"I trust you, and I trust April. No one else."

"You better remember that, Mick."

The Hotel Grand Westin
2200 hours

Mick opened the room door with some caution and stood there listening before he entered. He cautiously walked in, and after putting the heavy rifle in a corner, found Sasha asleep, curled on the big bed. The food trays were still covered and looked untouched. He threw his backpack on the bed and Sasha stirred.

"That you, Mick?" she said without moving.

"Didn't you eat?"

"I wanted to, but I fell asleep waiting for you.

Everything all right?"

"April still hasn't been found. They are still looking. Did you get the card into Danny's wallet?"

"No, better. I put it in the car under the front carpet when I was alone with the car."

"Sounds like you used your head instead of your body. I like it. Anyone see you?"

"Yes, the guards and Dmitri. The guards saw the false identification. Dmitri wouldn't dare admit that he saw me, because he didn't hold me for questioning. No one else saw me, and I took my time coming back here. We are safe for now."

She extended her arm and Mick gently pulled her to a sitting position. "Ready to eat some cold food?" he asked.

They took turns during the night watching the video monitor of the Russian Embassy exit ramp. The camera, wherever it was, gave a good view, both during the day and at night. They saw cars coming and going, but the red Mercedes limousine was not one of them. The morning came at last, and they were able to order coffee and breakfast to be sent up to the room.

"Mick, what are you going to do after this mission is over?" Sasha asked while they ate.

"As you know, I usually live around Tacoma, and I have a little private detective business. I will probably go back there and pick up the pieces."

"Are you planning to marry April Chauncy?"

"We are colleagues and partners, but I don't have a romance going with her, and we certainly have never discussed marriage."

"Aren't you attracted to me?" she asked, looking seductively over her shoulder.

"There isn't a man alive who wouldn't be attracted to you, Sasha. The last time we had this conversation, you got your feelings hurt and felt rejected. But my response is the same today. I can't think about anything but the mission, and romance is out of my scope right now. Please don't think that means that I don't find you attractive or desirable. You know that I have come to like you, and treat you with respect and tenderness, and you also know that I don't want anything bad to happen to you. We have to put aside anything which could interfere with the business at hand. Later. We will have this conversation later." Sasha produced a little pout and turned her face away so that he couldn't see her.

The day wore on, and shortly after lunch there was some new activity at the Russian Embassy. Cars started coming and going more frequently, and a couple of armed guards were standing at the entry way canvassing the street.

"We might have some action soon, Sasha. You better get some clothes on and get ready," Mick advised.

A red limousine slid out of the ramp smoothly onto the street. Mick hesitated to turn the tracking device on and waited. Another identical car came up the ramp and turned the opposite way. Since they both were out and moving, he triggered the signal to activate the device. A blip showed on the map, moving in the direction the first car took. "Let's go, Sasha. This is it."

Chapter 23

April's Capture

April took off before anyone could stop her. She quickly studied a map before leaving, memorizing the route to the *Schwerbelastungskörper*. Hurrying to catch Mick, she quickly realized that following his motorcycle was impossible. She had no plan of what to do when she got there, but she felt like she must be available to protect her partner, if possible. At least if he called her, she might be close enough to provide assistance. She knew that she couldn't live with herself if he were killed while she was sitting comfortably at the Embassy sipping coffee. A particular white car was following her, and she kept seeing it dart in and out of the other traffic. She was keeping an evermore watchful eye on the small white sedan when a large dark car passed her, unexpectedly pulling in front. Her foot reflexly braked hard to avoid a collision, as the following car closed up behind, while a third car stopped alongside. Before she could react, there was a man standing just outside of her window, aiming an automatic at her face. Another appeared in front of the car with a small machine gun pointed at her through the windshield. Someone jerked the car door open and roughly pulled her stumbling out into the street. She was about to protest and show her FBI badge when a fierce stabbing pain hit her in the back, and she lost consciousness.

When awakened, she was in a very dark place, lying face down with her hands tied behind her back with something sharp. She tried to move her feet and found that they were also tied. As she raised her head to look around, she could make out a room with little in it. There were no windows, the only available light filtering faintly under a single door. A small table and three chairs occupied the center of the room. She realized that she was covered with a sheet, but all her clothing had been removed. Muffled voices, which were neither German nor English, drifted under the door. Her lips were dry and cracked, and she was hungry. There was no way to determine how much time had passed since her capture. She rocked to her side and felt the cold concrete block wall behind her. After rolling over, she gave a lunge and folded into a sitting position, her covering sheet falling into her lap. She struggled a bit with her hands but could feel the restraint cutting into her skin. There seemed to be no options, and she was at the mercy of whoever had captured her. As she sat motionless, thinking, she became cold, but there was no way of covering herself again. The voices became louder, accompanied by the sound of something heavy being moved and keys rattling in a lock. A door creaked open, spilling light into her prison followed by two shadows, both were large and hulking. April saw that one was male, the other female, and they were dressed in rough clothes like workmen. She attempted to turn away to hide her nakedness but doing so was fruitless. Instead, she faced them defiantly.

"We find you awake, FBI," the female remarked in accented-English. They both grinned at her helplessness. April could feel the leering eyes of the male rake her body over and over.

"What do you people want? Why have I been imprisoned here?" April demanded.

The male said, "You are our captive. We give orders. You obey."

"How long have I been here?" April asked loudly.

"You write letter for us, and you get food. Agreed?" the female said.

"What letter? What do you want?"

"FBI not ready," the male determined. They shrugged at each other and headed back toward the door.

"Wait!" April demanded. "I need to use the toilet, and I need water. Also, I am cold."

"We know," one of them said before the door closed.

April was angry and struggled with her restraints. The ones on the ankles were simple but heavy gauge plastic slip ties. She assumed that the same kind was on her wrists, and she knew from experience that this kind cannot be broken and would cut deeply into the skin over time. A sharp knife would work, but there was nothing like that in the room. She looked a long time at the table and thought she could make out a paper and pen lying on the top.

They wanted her to write a letter for some reason. As she thought it out, there could be only one reason and that would be to convince someone that she was still alive. It dawned on her that it was meant for Mick Grundy. They were going to use her as the final tool needed to force Mick to assassinate Anatoly Baranov. That meant that Sinitsin's people were the ones who kidnapped her. Sasha had claimed that she was working for Sinitsin. April always knew that Sasha could not be trusted, and it was clear that she had to get away, because once Mick did the assassination, there would be no reason for them to keep her alive. Kidnapping her was enough to cause an international fracas, but silencing her would avoid it, because there would be no proof of who had captured her. The inescapable fact was that she was not going to get out of this room alive.

There was something going on in the next room. She could hear the excited voices and feet moving around. The door opened again, and the same couple came rushing into the room. They wasted no time in stuffing a small cloth into April's mouth, then using a liberal strip of duct tape over her mouth and around the back of her head.

The male leaned over her with his fetid breath and said, "Make no sound or you die." As he stood to leave, April heard the female say something incomprehensible, but one part was unmistakable, "Mick Grundy." From their looks of panic and the feverish movement, they were terrified. Mick must be close, she realized. She considered what to do. A concrete wall behind her would not sound out unless struck by a sledgehammer. She couldn't make any significant verbal cry, and the awful fact struck her that she could do nothing to attract his attention. The same heavy object was being moved again, meaning that the door to her cell was hidden by something. Someone entering the adjoining room may not find her, even if they were looking. She knew that if Mick entered he would intuitively know something was wrong. He could and would make those two talk, because they both were already afraid of him. April mentally willed Mick to come to her rescue, straining to the point of panic. Sadly, nothing happened, and the scuffling outside her room ceased. Mick had gone away without finding her. She started to cry and then wretch against the gag in her mouth.

Outside in the yard in front of her prison, Mick got the telephone call which pulled him away. He had been no more than twenty feet from April at the time. The two Russian guards were peering through cracks, in near panic, watching him. The male had a small pistol in his hand, but he knew he was no match for Mick Grundy. It was with great relief when they saw Mick walk away.

The female guard said, "We need to make her write the letter. This was our instructions. If we have the letter, we will need her no more, and we can leave her here and get away before this Mick Grundy returns. He is sure to kill us if he finds her."

The male guard agreed, "Yes, you are right. We may have to give in and let her use the toilet and feed her first. I will go out and get some food. You go in and release her, and let her use the toilet. Also, give her some water. I will return quickly. Be most careful, because she is a trained agent and likely can be dangerous."

"Why should you be the one who goes for food? How do I know you will return?" the female guard demanded.

"All right. You go for food. I will remain here with FBI," he said with a sly smile on his face.

The female guard said, "I thought you would start that sooner or later. I don't care what you do with her, just don't let her get away."

April could hear new noise outside the room, and again the heavy object started moving, keys clicked against the door. She rolled back to a sitting position and watched as the male came lumbering toward her. He was grinning as he violently pulled the tape from her mouth, pulling away some of her hair in the process. She spat out the wad from her mouth and glared at him. He reached down and cut her feet loose with a small pliers, then spun her around and cut her hands loose. He moved back from her and pulled his pistol as she stood up completely naked. He looked her up and down and motioned for her to turn around, wanting a full inspection of her from all sides. She stood there, defiantly facing him. They stood at an impasse for a moment, and then he motioned with his pistol and pointing, "Toilet," indicating the open door with his other hand. She walked ahead of him, and as she passed through the door, she could see the large cabinet that they had been sliding around to hide the door. The door to the toilet was open, and she started to close it behind her, but his foot prevented it. He watched in amusement as she relieved herself. She finished and stood up to face the man, his gun still pointed at her chest. The look on his face told her that she was about to be raped. Grinning and displaying his bad teeth, he motioned for her to return back into her cell. She walked with grace knowing the effect her body was having on him, letting her hips sway and move. His eyes were trapped and mesmerized by her moving buttocks. and he was no longer aware of anything she did other than move. She walked slowly up to the table holding the pen and paper and turned her back to it, facing him. His eyes wandered back and forth between her pubis and her breasts, never watching her face. If he had, he might have known what was coming. He closed the distance between himself and this irresistible woman, wanting to touch her and feel her female flesh in his hands. The pen swept up in a long arc with blinding speed and entered the side of his neck, just at the Adam's apple. The pen came out the other side of his throat and was followed by a kick to his groin which was as swift and even more painful. He fell to the floor gasping for breath, dimly aware that her hand removed the gun from his, but unable to do anything about it. The gunshot to his head was a relief for him, because his pain stopped abruptly.

April dragged the lifeless body from the center of the room and put it just to one side of the door so it would not be seen unless someone fully entered the room. She reasoned that the female would return, but whether anyone else would accompany her was the question. She looked outside through the cracks but saw only an empty parking lot and overhead, a darkened sky. She searched for her clothing, but it wasn't to be found in either of the two rooms. She considered removing the man's clothing but heard a noise outside the building that made her scurry for her room. She closed the door and waited behind it.

"Я вернулся с пищей. Я надеюсь, что вы закончили завинчивания ФБР сейчас. Я собираюсь приехать в настоящее время." ["I am back with the food. I hope you have finished screwing FBI by now. I'm going to come in now."]

The door opened abruptly, and the large mass of the female guard came in holding a bag. She looked around surprised and was about to say something when the gun exploded behind her left ear. She hit the floor with a crash, and her paper bag slid across the room. April stripped enough clothing from the woman to cover herself, finding the car keys she had just used. She put the handgun into an oversized pocket. There was no choice about being barefooted, because the woman's shoes were much too large. She dragged both heavy bodies farther into the back room and then locked the door from the outside and pushed the heavy cabinet in front. There was no sign of her imprisonment or of her captors in the outside room. Cautiously looking outside, she noted that darkness had come, and the parking lot seemed nearly empty. She walked outside and found the only car with a hot hood. Happily, the key fit, and as she pulled away, she noticed a line of police vehicles approaching the area. Finally, rescue had come, but she didn't want to stop and explain the dead bodies to the Germans. She decided to first seek the safety of the American Embassy, and let them explain for her.

April turned a corner and accelerated hard, the small engine groaning to keep up with her demands. She vaguely remembered where she had been before her capture, but she had been moved and kept in another area. She was lost. A huge clock embedded in a shadowy monumental building had its hands approaching two. She had no identification, no money and no telephone and began to wish that she had stayed to be interrogated by the German Police. Without warning, a siren started up just behind her and flashing lights indicated that a police car was following her. She pulled to the side and rolled down her window. A bright light shone into her face, and she noticed another policeman on the other side of the car.

"*Sie werden aus dem Auto bitte gehen,*" ["You will step out of the car, please,"] he said.

"I am sorry, I don't speak German," April said.

"Step out of the car, madam," he repeated.

April got out and the two patrolmen looked at her outfit with subdued amusement.

"What are you dressed for, madam?" the first one asked.

"I was held captive, and I had to borrow these clothes," she answered. The two officers were looking her over with their flashlights.

"*Ich sehe Bluttropfen,*" ["I see blood droplets,"] one

of the officers said. He reached out and patted her down and quickly found her pistol. He looked it over and smelled the barrel. *"Die Waffe ist kürzlich angezündet worden."* ["The weapon has been fired recently."] The officers removed the ignition key and opened the trunk. One of them removed an automatic weapon and a large amount of ammunition. They handcuffed her and led her back to the patrol car.

"Madam, you are going to be held pending investigation," the first officer said.

"But..." April blurted.

"You will have an opportunity to tell your story later. Now you must be quiet and cause us no problems," the officer warned.

They drove away with April in the back seat, handcuffed.

American Embassy, Berlin
1230 hours

Elmer Septer opened Zeskie's door and saw him looking intently at his computer screen. "Ron, I got a message from the Berlin police. They have a woman in custody who may be our April Chauncy. The are holding her downtown and are gearing up to charge her with two murders. They said that she is American and asking for help from the FBI and the American Embassy."

Zeskie didn't look up and said, "Well, the raid last night turned up two bodies in one of the flats. They were hidden in a small room. There was no trace of April, but they are running fingerprints, DNA and ballistics on the two bullets. My bet is that the woman they are holding is April. She'll have quite the story to tell. Want to accompany me down there and try to spring her?"

"I was planning on it. I have copies of her badge and passport to convince them. Could you also call your contacts at the BND and get them involved?" Septer asked.

1420 hours

Mick and Sasha were following the red limousine from a safe distance using the tracking device. The car took a wandering route but appeared headed in an easterly direction. Mick let Sasha drive while he studied the map and the signal. He looked at the terrain and landmarks ahead as progress was slowly made toward the east. Mick thought, where is a good place to have a meeting which is both private and secure? He jumped ahead with his finger and found the *Volkspark*. There were only two car entrances to the largely wooded public park. Once inside, the site would be easy to protect. Near the center of the park was a parking area and cafe. This was a perfect place to watch and to protect, with fewer people than any street location. He watched as the signal moved ever closer to the park and then turned onto Landsberger. There was no doubt. The meeting was going to be in *Volkspark*. As he watched intently, the signal made the turn onto *Ernst-Zenna* into the park. They were about a mile behind, and Mick started looking for a high place. He hoped that a church steeple or large building could be found, but this area of Berlin seemed void of very high structures.

"Stop, Sasha!" he ordered, and she braked hard, screeching to the curb. They were on *Otto-Braun Strasse* and roughly a mile from the center of the *Volkspark Friedrichshain*. He got out of the car and looked around. This was a good distance for the fifty caliber rifle but no high places to shoot from. The sun had begun to set and was behind them to the west. If he could spot a location in this area, the sun would prevent anyone in the park from seeing him or a muzzle flash when he took a shot. Mick felt more and more desperate as he scanned the horizon. He briefly considered a run into the park, attempting a shot through the trees. He knew that doing so would get him too close, and there was a danger that the alert bodyguards would spot him or anticipate him. Likely, the park was already full of armed men on the lookout for trouble. Then he saw it. Just ahead were twin towers of construction cranes. He watched for a moment and saw no motion. They weren't working today. Perfect. He got back in the car and looked at his map.

"Sasha, drive toward those two cranes just ahead." Instantly, Sasha knew what he was planning.

"You are going to do the assassination of Baranov after all, aren't you?" she asked.

"That is what we planned. Did you have doubts?"

"I wondered. What made you finally decide?"

"Capturing April. I couldn't leave her in their hands, and I don't know if they will release her as they promised, but if they don't, I will hunt them all down starting with Sinitsin."

Sasha had a tear run down her face, but Mick didn't notice. It seemed to her that no matter what she offered to Mick, he would always prefer April. Sasha realized that she was only a tool to everybody. A pretty little throwaway tool.

"Pull in here and wait for me," Mick said. They turned into a construction site, and there were a few workers in sight. Mick got out of the car and looked carefully at one of the crane towers. The tower rose at least three hundred feet. Near the top was a cabin that the operator used, and the jib which did the lifting, suspended horizontally in both directions. Mick could see no one in the tower. He waved to a worker who came his way.

"Ich muss mit dem Vorarbeiter oder Oberaufseher sprechen," ["I need to speak to the foreman or supervisor,"] Mick said. The man pointed to a fellow holding a clipboard and wearing a white hard hat. Mick walked over to him and waited for his attention.

"Ich muss eine Notreparatur zum Kran machen. Ich dachte, dass Sie jetzt sollten, bevor ich stieg. Es wird nicht lange dauern." ["I need to make an emergency repair to the crane. I thought you should know before I went up. It won't take long."] The foreman looked him over and nodded his consent and again started studying his clipboard.

Mick returned to the car where Sasha was waiting outside by the trunk. "I am going up to see if a shot is possible. If they see me or figure it out, they are going to come this way as fast as they can." He reached behind his back and discretely pulled out his 45 caliber pistol. "You take this and defend yourself if you have to. Use the car to get away if I can't get down in time. Save yourself. There is no reason for both of us to die." She tucked the weapon in her clothing and started to cry. She clung to Mick looking up at him.

"We could be so happy together, Mick, if you would try. Don't do this just because of April. Whatever happens to her is not your fault. Remember that we have each other. Let's leave this place together right now. Don't go up there, because if you do, there is no turning back."

Mick gently pushed her away and said, "You know I have to do this. I promise when I come down that we will talk about the future, but for now you must wait for me." He opened the trunk of the car and took out his backpack and the rifle in its black case and slung both over his back. He leaned down and kissed Sasha on the forehead and then turned toward the tower.

Chapter 24

The Shooting

Construction towers have no elevator and must be climbed one step at a time. The steps consist of a steel ladder going straight up inside the structure. Mick climbed as fast as he could, given the extra weight he was carrying. He panted for breath and gritted his teeth and pushed upward, leaving Sasha looking smaller and smaller as he rose. The park was coming in sight as he gained altitude, but it was too far away to discern cars or people. He would have to wait for the view through the telescopic sight. When he reached the cab, he realized that it would not give his rifle the view or room that he required, and he started sliding and working his way out on the horizontal jib. After about fifteen feet, he stopped and unpacked his backpack. He carried two long nylon climbing ropes and a variety of carabineers and rappelling devices. He quickly opened the ropes and tied the ends in a figure of eight, tying one end to the steel structure. The free end was left available. He quickly unpacked and set up the rifle and stretched out horizontally, assuming a firing position.

Mick got his first view of the *Volkspark,* finding the

Cafe Schoenbrunn sign with the scope and tracking toward the parking in front. The red limousine was parked in full view and stood alone with no other cars close by. He was in time, the meeting had not yet started. Mick loaded his weapon with the ammunition supplied by Shotgun. The bullets had an explosive tip and a tungsten penetrator which could punch through almost anything. No automobile armor could begin to stop one of these. Mick eased into a comfortable position and waited. He checked the distance to the red car. 1533.33 meters. It was well inside of the far targets on the range. There was no wind moving among the trees, and conditions were perfect for a clean shot. He glanced down and could see Sasha still waiting beside the car. After a couple of moments his breathing slowly returned to normal after his exhausting climb. There was something moving near the red car. A long black car with dark windows slid into view as two smaller black cars came up, parking nearby at defensive angles. Several husky men emerged from the second cars and started surveying the terrain. They were obviously well-trained and fit, and one of them was looking in Mick's direction with a pair of binoculars. The sun was directly behind Mick, and he was sure that he could not be seen. For a moment, nothing moved, then the red car's passenger door opened, and a tall thin man wearing a dark suit emerged. Flanked by two of the security men, he was accompanied to the large dark car. The man entered the black car on the side away from Mick, and the door closed behind him. Two men waited by the hood of the car, ever vigilant. Mick realized that he was not going to get a clean shot at Baranov this way. When the meeting was over, Viktor Asmonov would simply get out and walk back to his car, and Baranov would be driven away. Mick had to change things. He remembered that at this distance the flight time of the bullet would be just under two seconds. Targets can move around a lot in two seconds. He needed the object stationary to be sure to hit it.

Taking aim at the black car, he located the strike zone at the ten o'clock position of the front tire, which would cause the bullet to hit the motor, disabling the car. Spitting flame and ear shattering noise, the gun fired and the hood of the car was carried upward by the explosion. He quickly aimed for the probable location of the gas tank at the rear of the car and fired. A small fireball erupted underneath the car and flames spread quickly behind and on the side away from Mick's vision. The only exit was the door toward Mick. Two men rushed to the rear passenger door and, with their bodies, were attempting to block any fire coming toward their boss. Mick caught a glimpse of the top of Baranov's head. It was him. Mick fired two quick shots, one at his head and one at the probable location of his body as he was emerging from the car. The impact of the exploding bullet propelled the three men back into the rear seat, just as the car was engulfed in flames. Mick sighted on one of the accompanying car's engine blocks before they realized that they had to move the car out of the firing zone. One after another, the cars exploded at the front end, sending up sheets of flame. The big red limousine was starting to leave, and Mick fired two shots leading it as if it were a duck or clay target. It also exploded, sending the hood into the air nearly thirty feet. When he took a last look at the scene, there were several men pointing in his direction. He knew that he couldn't be seen, but understood that the well-trained Russians may have guessed the location of his firing platform. Putting the rifle away quickly, he tied into the rope with his rappelling device and tossed the free end toward the ground. He lowered himself straight down the rope reaching the knot in the middle, then tied another device below the knot, quickly dropping into the parking lot.

Sasha was waiting outside the car and leaning into it in a casual way. Her head was down, and she looked at him with darkness in her eyes. "Get in, Sasha. They will be coming soon. We have to get away from here!" She didn't move, and he gave her a longer look. "Didn't you hear me? We don't have much time. Get in the car," he ordered. He opened the trunk and threw the rifle in, and when he stood up, he saw that Sasha was pointing his gun at him. Tears streamed down her face, and the gun was trembling. "Sasha?" Mick questioned. "I don't understand?" A nearby pistol cracked twice, and Sasha fell forward into the dirt. Mick looked up to see April lowering her pistol. He jumped to Sasha and gently turned her over. There was dark blood oozing from two sites, one from her chest and the other her abdomen. Her eyes fluttered, and she looked into Mick's face.

"I was ordered to kill you, Mick. I didn't want to, but I finally realized that when this was over, you would leave me, and I would have nothing. At least if I killed you, I could go back to Russia."

"Oh, Sasha, I would have looked after you. You beautiful, beautiful child. Such a waste." He put his arms behind her and elevated her upper body supporting her head.

"Something you should know, Mick," she whispered. He leaned closer. "Sinitsin is not your father. He lied to you. He is my father." Her eyes became distant, and Mick could feel her relax. After gently lowering her to the ground, he saw a shadow come up just behind him, and he knew it was April. He stood up without taking his eyes from Sasha.

"Sorry it had to end that way, Mick," April said and touched his arm. I had no choice but to kill her or to watch her kill you." Mick bent down and picked up his 45 caliber pistol.

"It wasn't loaded. I gave her an empty gun," he said.

April put her hands to her mouth and gasped. "Oh no! I didn't have to shoot her." She bent forward in agony, turning away from Mick. He enveloped her from the back and spoke into her ear. "You did what you felt you had to do, April. Sasha did this to herself. Thank you for saving my life." He slowly turned her around and kissed her hard and passionately on her lips and her wet face.

"If we don't get away from here pronto, we will have to shoot our way out. Let's go." He led her by the arm to the car, and they drove away, leaving Sasha lying in the dirt looking up at the sky. A small crowd of workers gathered beside the body as two cars came roaring up, and men with machine guns emerged looking wild and angry.

Chapter 25

Another Hunt

American Embassy, Berlin
1620 hours

Emerging from the car in the underground garage, Mick went to the other side and helped April out. She was devastated because Sasha was killed holding an empty gun, shot in the back without warning. They had not spoken during the ride back to the Embassy, except when Mick told her that he was glad she was safe, and that he appreciated her efforts on his behalf. She was unable to answer and cried silently most of the way back, her face in her hands.

"April, I don't yet know what happened to you when you were captured, but I assume that it was ugly. You need to have some down time while the rest of the loose strings are tied up."

"You mean that there is more you have to do?"

"There is Sinitsin to deal with. I can't let him go unpunished," Mick said.

"I am free, Mick, and I am unharmed. There is no need for any further action. Let it go. Please," April said, and her tears started forming again.

Ron Zeskie came up and put his arm around April. "Dear, Miss Chauncy. Excuse me. Dear Special Agent Chauncy. You have had a busy day. We never had our debriefing, and I don't think you have eaten anything in days. You need to come with me. Elmer is waiting for you." He looked over at Mick and said, "Mick, we need to talk. Give me a moment to take care of this wonderful example of strength and courage. Go up to my office and wait for me."

Mick watched as Zeskie led April away. His arm was over her shoulder, and he leaned his head into hers. Mick did as asked and went to his office and poured himself a cup of coffee, collapsing into a soft chair. As he thought over the recent events, he grew angrier by the moment. Sinitsin had lied about everything, and even threw away his own daughter just to advance himself and his career. There was really no way of knowing what would have happened to April if she hadn't escaped, but Mick doubted if Sinitsin ever intended to let her go. Sasha was assigned to kill Mick after the hit, just as April always said. He allowed himself to think about Sasha and closed his eyes remembering colored lights dancing on her face outside the casino in Las Vegas. Of course he was attracted to her, and he had grown to trust her and think of her as part of a team. She was always going to be Sinitsin's daughter, though, and she would have been pulled back into his world eventually. On this, Sasha was right. There was no hope for a real relationship between them, and it had ended as it was destined to end.

The door exploded open, and Zeskie entered in a

hurry. "Listen, Mick, April needs you, but first we have to talk. The news about your shooting fit is all over the place. We have put a spin on it and blamed it on infighting among the Russians, which is essentially true, but I'm sure the Russians are hearing a different story from Sinitsin. He will name you as the assassin and claim that you had help from the CIA. Expectedly, he will point to the death of his daughter to prove his innocence, and he will vow to bring you to justice. We watched as his car and retinue rolled triumphantly into the Russian Embassy shortly ago. My bet is that he will know that you are coming for him, and he will try to get away from Berlin as soon as possible. You can expect that he will leave with an impressive armed escort."

"Suggestions?" Mick asked dryly.

"Well, if you just flee, escaping in the middle of the night so to speak, you will be back in the same game of hiding from killers the rest of your short life. However, if you rid the planet of Sinitsin, there are sure to be some of his people who will tell the true story. My advice is to finish this thing, but don't tell anyone I said it."

"Assuming you are right about Sinitsin trying to leave quickly, where and how will he go?"

Zeskie rocked back in his chair with his arms behind his head, looking at the ceiling. "He knows, as we all know, that you are an expert sniper and that you can kill from a great distance. If he goes to the airport, you could be waiting and do the same thing to the airplane or to the car which brings him, and you could do it from a safe distance. Trains are out for the same reason. If I were him, I would rapidly conclude my business at the Embassy and get out of Dodge. If he leaves before you can get ready, he might get away. Following this line of reasoning, if he travels due east toward Mother Russia, he would be a sitting target at some point, assuming you can get ahead of him. No, I would head south at high speed on the Autobahn to a Bavarian city and catch a private plane which could already be waiting for him. Yes. He will head south and soon."

Mick turned the computer around to face him and brought up a map of Germany. "Normally, you would expect him to head toward Warsaw, but given your expectations, he will go south. Let's see...Nuremberg, Munich?"

"Munich. The Russians have an active office there. They would see to it that a plane is waiting at the large Munich airport. It's got to be the one."

"Well, how are we going to know, Zeskie?" Mick asked.

Zeskie sat up and turned the computer back around to face him. He clicked on the keys furiously and then sat back again. "Simple. We will watch his car by satellite when it leaves the Embassy. We will track it for a while to get the vector and then it's all yours, Mick."

Mick thought about this plan for a moment, and then said, "If he goes south, can you get Master Sergeant Charles Willford Howard of the sniper training school to call me?"

"Getting the U.S. Army involved, Mick?" Zeskie

said, looking worried.

"No. It's not killing that will be required. Shotgun may be able to stop or slow the caravan until I get there."

"Shotgun? Well, there's a name. Why him?" Zeskie wondered.

"We hit it off, and he offered to help. He is the chief instructor and a master with a sniper rifle. By the way, he only knows me as *Oberst* Brauer, but you can tell him my real name now."

"Settled then. Go and be with April. I'll set things up and call you when I know anything.

Mick found April in a small private lounge watching television with an uneaten plate of food in front of her. She was by herself, and when he looked carefully at her, he could still see that her eyes were red from crying. "Hi. Would it be okay to talk to you a bit?" he asked. She patted the couch beside her but said nothing. The television station she had on was a German one with only the German language being spoken. "Learning German?" Mick joked. As he sat down, she twisted and enveloped him in a hug. She buried her face in his chest and just held on. Her hair was in his face, and he smoothed it away. "I want to know what happened to you and how you came to be in the right place at the right time," he said softly.

It took a few moments for April to release him, and she patted her eyes and nose with a small handkerchief. "I am not sure how long I was held. They drugged me and kept me in a small room. I ended up shooting both of them to get away. The police arrested me and took me to a lock up, but I must say that they were most courteous and efficient. After about seven hours, Elmer and Ron came down, but the man who really got me out was the Director of the BND, Gunther Weisman. He came to the police station personally, and he brought a change of clothes. When the police let me go, Gunther gave me the keys to his own car as well as his personal weapon and told me where you were. I went straight there using the car's navigation system."

Mick frowned, "I won't even guess how they knew where I was. It would seem impossible."

"Mick, tell me the truth. If I had gotten there sooner, would you have shot Baranov? Did you do it just to get me free?" she asked.

Mick looked at her for a long time as if he were deciding what to tell her. "Yes, you were a large part of the decision. At the same time, I knew that they didn't intend to let you go, just as I knew in my heart that someone would try to kill me afterward. I hoped that it wasn't Sasha, and I was disappointed to find out that it was."

April held Mick tight and said, "What is troubling me the most is that I hated Sasha for her attraction to you and your attraction to her. I was jealous. The question that keeps playing over and over in my mind is did I shoot her partly for jealousy or just to protect you?"

"I think that you acted to save my life at the time, and you didn't even think past that. You did what you have been trained to do. Either way, it is a profound compliment to me. I hope that I can live up to and be worthy of what you did for me."

Mick's phone rang. Before he picked it up, he knew that it was Zeskie, and he knew that he would soon be on the hunt again. "Yes? I'll be right there." He looked at April and hated to tell her the truth. "Something has come up, April. I'll return as soon as possible," he said, kissing her on the forehead.

"No amount of begging will make you stay here, Mick?"

"Get some rest and food, April. I promise that I'll come back," he said, closing the door behind him.

Zeskie was still staring at his computer screen when Mick came in. "Well, just as we thought, Sinitsin is on the move and heading south. His group just passed the Berlin city limits. They are on the A100 now and soon will connect with the A115. After that, I'm betting on the A10, then the A9. Nearly straight south. If they stay on this Autobahn to Nuremberg, they will pass only 20 miles from *Grafenwöhr* training base. I just put in a call to your friend, Shotgun. He should call back shortly." Zeskie cleared his throat and continued, "Here is what you are facing. There are five cars in the group, and all are black. Two cars in front of the limo, two cars following. We can't tell what is in the cars as far as manpower, but expect the worst...heavily armed Spetsnaz."

Mick's phone rang. "Hello, Mick Grundy. This is Shotgun. I hear that you need my help, and I am here to give it to you."

"Hi, Shotgun. I have a big challenge ahead, and I

do need a good shooter. Can you get off the base in about three hours and bring a 50 caliber with you?' Mick asked.

"Can be done, will be done, my friend. What then?"

"There is a five car armada of Russians coming your way. I want the man riding in the limo, which will be in the middle. They are going to pass near *Grafenwöhr* using the A9. You should try to intersect them just before they get to Bayreuth. You are to take out the last two cars. If the first two cars stop, take them out also. Leave the limo to me. I am coming your way on my motorcycle, and we will coordinate after I get closer. It will be dark by then, so you will need a night scope. Got it?"

"I'll be there, Mick. Count on it," Shotgun said.

Chapter 26

The Chase

A Hilltop Overlooking Autobahn A9 Near Bayreuth
2130 hours

Shotgun and his spotter, Sergeant Raymond LaToya, parked the Humvee out of sight in the woods and gathered their gear. Shotgun had chosen a long barreled version of the Barrett 50 caliber rifle and attached a large night scope. He had sighted it in quickly before packing it away. Ray was carrying a large night vision telescope and packing a lightweight 30 caliber machine gun with a can of ammo. Both men were heavily laden and both wore Ghillie suits. They made their way silently through the light forest and selected a hillside which gave a good view of the Autobahn. Shotgun wanted to be as close as reasonable because of the speed of the cars he wanted to hit, choosing a site only 400 meters from the edge of the highway. The cars he was requested to stop could be packed with experienced men who would emerge near to his position. The machine gun was a last resort, and Shotgun was depending on their near invisibility in the Ghillie suits. They took their time digging in and added local camouflage consisting of leaves and twigs to their suits. After assuming a shooting position, they were nearly invisible from far away or close.

American Embassy
1810 hours

Mick attached the case with the sniper rifle to his motorcycle and pulled on his black racing suit and black helmet. He studied the map carefully before starting his motor. Assuming that the parade of cars that he pursued would be traveling as fast as possible, he calculated that he would catch them in just over two hours. That would put him close to Bayreuth where Shotgun was supposed to start shooting. Mick wanted to arrive while the Russians were disoriented and before they could get backup in place. Before he left, Mick attached a communicator to his helmet which worked in conjunction with his cell phone, allowing him to take and receive calls without stopping. There is no speed limit enforced on the Autobahn, something Germany is famous and infamous for, and tonight that ability to go fast will pay off, Mick thought.

The motorcycle headed smoothly up the ramp and away from the Embassy. Once he got on the wide divided highway system, he aggressively increased speed. When traffic allowed, he opened up the bike, reaching nearly 300 kilometers per hour. He made rapid progress and reached the southern directional A9 quickly, maintaining speeds well over 250 kilometers per hour most of the time. About 2230 hours, he received a telephone call from Shotgun.

"Hi, Mick, this is Shotgun. Are you headed this way?"

Mick responded. "Yes, I am, and making good time. Are you in position?"

"We are here, and we are ready for bear," he laughed.

"Shotgun, I don't want you to have to kill anyone, but you also have to protect yourself. Do what you have to do, and we will get out of it later, somehow."

"Don't worry about our safety. We have a fixed mount 30 caliber machine gun set up. No one could take our position easily."

Alexander Sinitsin's Limousine
2215 hours

They had been traveling for nearly four hours. Sinitsin insisted on more speed, but the caravan had been crawling along at about 150 kilometers per hour. Looking nervously behind the car, all he saw were the two following units full of big men. He reasoned that Grundy would expect him to go due east using the fastest route out of Germany, but he had better ideas. They would to go south instead. There was no way Grundy could figure out this plan in time. He briefly thought about little Sasha. Regrettable. She was useful, but in the end, was a failure as he feared would happen. Grundy was still alive. The way he had taken out Baranov was masterful and messy. But brilliant. Too bad he was on the other side. Sinitsin heard that the two oafs guarding the FBI agent had been killed and wondered if Grundy had been involved. It was hard to believe that one little woman could get the better of two experienced agents. It had to be Grundy. He checked behind the car again. How would Grundy be traveling, he wondered? He looked suspiciously at every car that they passed, wondering if he would see a gun before it fired at him. He began to sweat again. No, he told himself, this worked perfectly. We got rid of Baranov, and now I am in charge. Grundy is still alive, but we will eventually get him, and I will get the credit. He smiled to himself at his masterful plan, but his thoughts stopped when he heard a noise behind them. He looked back and saw that one of his cars was being left behind and was on fire. Sinitsin's driver was chattering with someone, and the limousine lurched forward in a sudden burst of speed when the driver's foot pressed the accelerator to the floor. He looked behind again just in time to see the hood of the other following car fly into the air. Before he could react or think he noticed that his car was passing both of the leading cars. They had slowed to render assistance to the other team members.

"No! Tell them not to stop! Quickly, get them back up with us!" Sinitsin yelled. As he looked back, he saw each car lose control as a ball of fire came from their front, and each car in turn went careening into the woods trailing a huge tongue of flame. He was alone with his limousine and the meaning was clear. Grundy was close by and pointing his finger of death at them.

According to the road signs, Mick was nearly at Bayreuth, and he cut his speed and sat up more alert. The telephone rang, and Shotgun's voice came over. "OK, Mick, we have taken four cars out. There were some injuries of the occupants, but what is worrisome is that they are swarming around like hornets looking for us. If they get any closer, we are going to open up on them."

"I am almost there. If they see me, they will suppose that I got away from them, and they will quit looking. Hang on."

Around the next bend, Mick could see a burning car by the side of the highway. In the shadows, he could see silhouettes of movement from several nearby men. As he got closer, he saw three cars which had gone out of control, crashing into the woods, also burning ferociously. He slowed, flipping his face shield up to get a better look. Several men were looking intently at him, and he could feel the hostility. He slowed even more, and when he got opposite them, he gave them a fist up, shaking it in the air and then accelerating hard. Sparks flickered on the highway as bullets fired at him struck the pavement. The motorcycle quickly reached top speed, pulling him safely out of range.

The phone rang again. "Thanks, partner," Shotgun said. "Your little wave did it, and they have assembled back on the highway. Looks like they are waiting for a ride. Watch out, because when they get one, they will head your way."

"Roger that. Thanks, Shotgun. You two withdraw when it's safe. I owe you one."

"Anytime, Mick."

Sinitsin looked behind the car again. "Faster, we need to go faster, driver," he screamed.

The driver looked in the rearview mirror and said calmly, "Sir, this vehicle has a top speed of 200 kilometers. That is in perfect conditions and not at night on a public highway. I am going as fast as is safe right now. There is nothing that I can see...." He stopped in mid-sentence as he watched a single bright light behind him grow larger. "Sir, is your assailant possibly on a motorcycle?"

"Of course he is. Haven't you heard the stories about Grundy?" Sinitsin shouted.

"Then, he is right behind us and gaining fast," the driver said.

Mick saw the taillights in front of him grow larger. He was making at least double the speed of the limousine, and he started to throttle down. He felt his back for his 45, and he glanced behind him for threats. The road was empty. Accelerating suddenly, he came up right behind the car, with his high beam on. The terrified face of Sinitsin looked back at him through the back glass. Other than the driver, Mick could see no one else in the car. The big car discharged a puff of grey smoke from the exhaust pipe and increased its speed. The head in the rear seat kept twisting to look back at Mick. He could see Sinitsin waving his fist at the driver. The speed increased, and Mick's speedometer hovered at nearly 200 kilometers per hour. Fast, very fast for such a big and clumsy car but slow for a motorcycle such as Mick was riding. He twisted the throttle hard, and the bike shot up beside the black limousine. Mick pulled his handgun from his back in full view of the rear seat passenger. The car roared and picked up more speed. The roadside signs indicated a turn to the left ahead. Mick dropped a safe distance behind the car, watching. He could see Sinitsin's fist beating on the glass between him and the driver. Mick dropped back a bit more to see what would happen as the road curved. The speed of both vehicles was still 150 kilometers or more. Mick watched as smoke poured from the car's tires as they engaged the pavement, clawing at the turn. The limo became unstable, twitching back and forth as it twisted its way through the turn. Suddenly, the back end lost traction, violently spinning the long car in a counter clockwise direction. Mick applied his brakes hard as the limo slew back around clockwise in the road, instantly starting to roll. The tumble was spectacular, and amid sparks and parts flying around, the car managed to align with the road briefly before beginning to topple end over end. After all forward momentum was spent, it came to rest upside down in a drainage ditch alongside the road. Mick stopped and got off the motorcycle, allowing his headlight to point toward the wreckage. White smoke poured out of the car's hood area, and in the silence, he could hear hot metal popping as it contracted. Mick peered into the dark car but could see nothing moving. Out of the darkness, there was a soft groan.

"Sinitsin, can you hear me?" Mick asked.

"Mick Grundy, what have you done?" the voice croaked.

Mick knelt down beside the window and tried to

look in. In the light from his motorcycle headlamps, he could just make out Sinitsin's form. "It was bound to end this way, Sinitsin, one way or the other. I heard Sasha say that she was your daughter just before she died. You treated her badly. She could have been a fine woman, but you compelled her to be a spy and then threw her away. You deserve this."

"Yes, that is true. My reach exceeded my grasp. At last you are free from all of us, my son....." The voice trailed off, and Mick could hear that the rough breathing had stopped. There was an absolute silence about the place, as if death had come and covered the area with his blanket. Mick listened to the sound of his footsteps in the gravel as he went back to his waiting motorcycle.

Chapter 27

The Ride Back

Mick decided that he would avoid the return trip past the waiting Russian guards, and he turned off the Autobahn at Bayreuth and made his way north and east knowing that he would run into the sprawling *Grafenwöhr* training base. It didn't take long before he encountered a guarded gate house at one of the entrances. He stopped short of the barricaded gate, shutting the bike down and called Shotgun on his phone.

"Shotgun here, that you Mick?" his voice said.

"I am at the south gate. Want to come take this rifle back from me? I'm done with it."

"Glad to hear your voice, Mick. Everything go all right then?"

"Didn't have to shoot anyone tonight. The limousine tried to outrun me and crashed. The man I was after died in the accident. It's over."

"I'll be right there. Don't go anywhere," Shotgun said.

The battered Humvee could be heard in the night air long before it was visible. It slid to a halt in a cloud of dust, and two men stepped out. They came across the guard gate with a wave to the MPs.

When Shotgun got close enough, he and Mick exchanged a manly embrace with back slapping. "This is Sergeant Raymond LaToya. Sometimes we call him Ray or Toy, depending on our mood," Shotgun said.

Mick stuck out his hand and said, "Good to meet you, Sergeant. Thanks for the help tonight. I couldn't have done it without you. Good shooting, you two. It was quite a sight seeing those four cars burning when I came through."

"Let met tell you, Mick, those guys were lucky that you came past and distracted them. They were almost on top of us, and they seemed to sense we were close. One foot more and we were going to take down the lot of them," Ray said.

"Well, it was better that we didn't have to explain a lot of dead bodies along the Autobahn. As it is, we can just laugh it off and deny it ever happened," Mick said. He went to his bike and unstrapped the rifle. "Take this thing back, Shotgun, and with my thanks. It worked like magic, but I won't need it again, at least on this trip."

Shotgun took it from him and winked, "I'll put your name on it for next time. It'll be here and so will we, anytime you need help."

Mick rolled down the long road back to Berlin. He was in no hurry, cruising along at a comfortable speed after deciding to take the smaller roads back, and prolonging the trip intentionally. Listening to the smooth motor and having the night air rush past him was hypnotic. He felt free for the first time in years. Perhaps now they would quit pursuing him, and he hoped he could return to a normal life. Again, his mind recalled Sasha, the beautiful, alluring Sasha. He sighed, remembering her voice and face and the way she would look between his eyes and his mouth when he spoke to her as if she were visually caressing his face. "Damn Sinitsin to hell," he thought out loud. Gripping the throttle in anger caused the bike to increase speed quickly. His thoughts came back to the present, and he backed off and fell to a reasonable speed. What did he feel for her, and what would have happened had things turned out differently? Realizing that he had not let himself think this way when he was with her made it difficult to be sure what he actually intended. A sexual fling with her had been out of the question, because he knew that it would cloud his judgment. He was the kind of man who didn't desire casual sex with a woman, instead preferring to possess her completely, inside and out. Most of all, he wanted a mental bond with a woman that was more, much more, than just a sexual act. He could not have achieved that depth with Sasha, because love has to start with not only lust but complete trust. He never did have complete trust in Sasha. There was always her mission and her training hanging around like a dark cloud. He realized that Sasha was right believing that he would have kept his word, insuring she was safely settled in America, but would never have settled down with her. She would have been left on her own just as she thought. He could summon no ill feeling for Sasha intending to shoot him to regain her position with her people. In a way, he deserved it, never telling her the raw truth, because he couldn't bring himself to think it through. What a waste of a beautiful woman, though. He raised his visor a bit to get fresh air, and the resultant noise distracted his thoughts. Taking a cleansing deep breath, he decided not to think about things he couldn't change. No matter what he had done or how this adventure unfolded, destiny insured an unfortunate outcome between himself and Sasha.

Mick pulled in for a fuel stop and shut the bike down. He was still vibrating and stiff from riding through the cold air. For the first time in recent memory, he didn't check out the surroundings for threats, he just gassed up the bike, used the restroom and paid like a normal person, feeling light on his feet like a huge weight had been lifted. There was no anger left in him and no fear of the future. He accelerated back onto the highway, feeling the joy of being alive come back inside, like his body was occupied by an alien. Now that his mind was clear, he realized that Zeskie and April and everyone he knew were waiting for him to come back. Zeskie was right. A lot of people cared about him. He started pushing the big bike harder, wanting to return and start his new life as soon as possible.

The motorcycle idled smoothly back into the underground parking at the Embassy. One of the guards gave him a big wave and smile, making him feel like he was coming home. He pulled off the helmet and leather suit and left them on the bike.

Wherever the machine came from he never knew, but he was finished with it, and they could have it back. Mick exploded up the stairs three at a time instead of using the elevator. He was stripped down to his pullover black shirt and his jeans, the butt of his 45 sticking out above his belt at the small of his back. First he stopped by Zeskie's empty office, then continued to the cafeteria, looking around but finding no one that he knew. He stood there wondering where April and Zeskie could be, when a guard tapped him on the shoulder.

"Mr. Grundy?"

"That's me."

"I have been asked to escort you to a conference room. This way, please," he said. Mick compliantly followed him down a long corridor to an area of the Embassy that he had not seen. At the end of the hall were two large decorative doors, and at this entrance, the guard stopped. "Here we are, sir. You are to go inside." The guard gave him a short salute and a smile and walked away.

Mick pushed on the doors, and they opened to a crowd of smiling faces gathered around a large table full of drinks and food. The applause started and they were all looking at him. April and Zeskie were standing together. His grandmother and brother in-law were there, and standing behind them with a big grin was his brother, Peter. Elmer Septer and Director Gunther Weisman were in the company of four Marines dressed in their best uniforms. Two unknown men attired in dark suits were also smiling at him.

Someone yelled, "Toast!" and the entire crowd picked up a champagne glass and held it in the air. "To Mick Grundy," the voice said, and they all took a sip at once and started cheering. Mick couldn't help but to wipe away a tear or two with the back of his hand. He just smiled back at each of them. April came to him first and put her arm behind his back. She turned him toward her with gentle pressure and tilted her head back and looked into his eyes. Without knowing what he was doing, he pulled her toward him and kissed her lips and held her tight. The crowd cheered again and raised their glasses, breaking toward him and surrounding him with pats and shakes. Each person in turn came to him for well wishes and a handshake. Last was Gunther Weisman, who clasped his hand and shoulder at the same time.

"Mick Grundy, I don't really know if you are a German or American, and I don't care. I know that you are one of us, and I would welcome it if you should choose to settle here. We are proud of you, and you will always have our friendship." Weisman didn't seem to want to let Mick's hand go, and he continued speaking in a sincere tone, "I have someone whom I want you to meet!" He let Mick go and placed his hand on the shoulder of one of the two men unknown to Mick.

"This is the new Director of the GRU in Berlin. Director Tostoroff, meet the infamous Mick Grundy." The man stepped forward and smiled at Mick and extended his hand.

"Mr. Grundy. I want to personally thank you for

ridding Russia of these two tyrants. Both were evil people and impossible to rid ourselves of from the inside. It took the courage and skill of someone outside like you to do what we couldn't do. Thank you from the bottom of my heart. I truly believe that relations between our three countries will improve now, and I wish to extend a warm welcome to you if you ever should want to visit our Mother Russia. The Premier himself also extends you this invitation and will give you a personal audience. He says to tell you that there are none in Russia who wish you any ill will over things that have happened in the past. We bear you no animosity, and we hold for you a position of deep respect."

Mick took his hand and shook it. They were eye to eye and as far as Mick could tell, Tostoroff was telling the truth. He felt a tap on the shoulder and turned.

"Mick Grundy, I am Rudimer Vostoff, assistant to the Russian Ambassador to Germany. I want to welcome you back to the safety of your friends which include me and my office. We extend to you every well wish for happiness, and if my office can ever assist you in any way, please call upon us." He also stuck out his hand and shook Mick's with sincerity.

Mick embraced Triska and kissed her on the forehead. She wrapped her arm around his waist and in the other arm held April. She looked back and forth between them and said, "You two look perfect together. There could be no better match. Though I do feel sorry for the one who takes the first swing in an argument."

They both chimed in, "That will never happen!"

Peter Koffman gave Mick his big embrace, picking him off the floor. "Brother! I am so happy that you came back to us. Never again put yourself at risk. You are all I have, and I can't lose you! Now, can I be best man at your wedding?" He gave a big laugh and slapped Mick on the back.

"Sorry to disappoint you, Brother. First, I need a bride. You remember that a woman has to say yes first?"

Peter looked at April's smiling face. "That won't be real hard, Brother. Say, there is something I need to tell you." His face became serious, and he pulled Mick aside. "We collected tissue from both Sasha and Sinitsin as well as Baranov. As is our custom, we are going to run comparative DNA of all of them. The question is...do you want to know the results?"

"No, Peter. I'm not ready for that. Perhaps someday you can tell me what you find, but not now."

"I thought as much," Peter said. "I don't blame you, Mick. The other thing is that Director Weisman has taken a personal interest in identifying our parents and tracing our origins. He has a team working on it right now. I assume that you want to hear how we are related when the results come in?"

"Same answer, Peter. I guess that I'm afraid to find the truth, because I feel happy right now for the first time since Anna died, and I don't want to discover anything that would change that. Just knowing you and knowing that we are brothers is enough. It makes me grateful just to be able to reach out and touch you."

"If you bring me to tears in front of Director Weisman, I will hate you for it," Peter said confidentially and wiped his eyes with his sleeve.

Outside the American Embassy, Berlin

A man with a hard sharp face was leaning against a stone wall of a building across the street from the entrance to the American Embassy. He wore a small earpiece which was nearly invisible. After puffing deeply on his cigarette, he looked around, then asked, *"Вы в положении?"* ["Are you in position?"]

The ear piece crackled, *"Да, команда находится в месте. Как долго делают мы должны стоять здесь? Мы выглядим подозрительными."* ["Yes, the team is in place. How long do we have to stand here? We look suspicious."]

"Пока требуется для него, чтобы выйти." ["As long as it takes for him to come out."]

The End